easy virtue,

mia asher

Editor: Jennifer Roberts-Hall
Cover Designer: Regina Wamba, Mae I Design
Interior Designer: Kassi's Kandids-Formatting
Proofreader: Ryn Hughes

easy virtue.

Always follow
your heart!

This is for you. **Thank You.**

If nothing saves us from death, may love at least save us from life.

~Pablo Neruda.

part one.
innocence
past

chapter one.

WHAT IS LOVE?

I don't know.

I've never had it.

Is it even real?

No, I don't think so. I mean, how can I believe in love when I've never witnessed it? When it seems to only exist in books and films, or in the lives of people more fortunate than me? *Trust me, I know.*

Love is my personal chimera.

I am gazing at brown eyes, admiring the richness of the color, the beauty of the man to whom they belong.

"You're so beautiful, Blaire ... so wet," he murmurs, his hand going between my legs as he begins to rub me. The soft invasion of his fingers spreads me open, tuning my body to his wants and needs, preparing me to be taken as the hot friction of his touch lights a wildfire within my body. It's not the first time he has touched me like this, but each time feels better and better—the sensations all consuming and heady.

One finger.

Two fingers.

One finger.

Two fingers.

Over and over again.

His invasion is fast and slow, deep and shallow. His touch is soiled heaven.

As I open my legs wider for him, I wonder if it feels this good because of him, or because I'm taking something that doesn't belong to me and making it mine.

"Don't stop … it feels so good," I breathe.

Okay, maybe it's because at this moment in time *this man* thinks he loves me and no one else but me, however false his proclamation may be.

I close my eyes as his lips land on mine. He kisses me gently, as if I'm made out of glass. He kisses me with that familiar mouth I've seen smile tenderly at me so many times before. The assault of his tongue debilitates me but doesn't incapacitate me.

"It's four dollars, gorgeous," the cute barista says, smiling at me.

I'm about to pay for my cappuccino when I hear a deep, manly voice say, "Let me get that for you."

A man wearing a beige suit comes forward, standing next to me as he hands the barista some bills. "I've seen you around … you're Paige's friend."

I smile, licking my suddenly dry lips. "Thank you, and yes … I know Paige."

The smile on his handsome face seems to freeze as his gaze follows the tip of my tongue, the spark of hunger brightening his eyes. Inwardly, I smile because who knew it was so easy to make men desire me, particularly when I went without attention for so long.

"My pleasure. Are you"—he coughs—"here with someone else?"

I shake my head and look at him through fluttering eyelashes. "No, I'm here by myself." I pause, touching his arm invitingly, and smile. "Would you like to join me?"

He looks around the coffee shop, probably considering if he should, if it's proper to do so, but less than five seconds later, he's staring at me once again. "Sure."

Yes, just like that.

The beige walls are spinning.

The clock is ticking.

The bed springs creak as the moon shines outside the motel window.

And the man above me kisses me while he fingers me, preparing me for him. *Gotta love such a thoughtful man.*

I can taste his sweet saliva mixing with mine, and I love it.

"Please," I beg against his lips, reaching for his hard cock and wrapping my fingers around it. "I'm ready."

I feel his mouth leave mine as he begins to make his way down my partially dressed body. "Are you sure, Blaire? Are you sure you want to do this with me?"

I open my eyes to witness what I think I want him to do. No, what I'm *sure* I want him to do. I can't help the smile I feel playing on my lips as I see him struggling with his conscience. He asks me if I'm sure when he has already fucked my mouth with his cock countless number of times, when his fingers have filled every orifice of my body. Should I laugh? No … I decide to take pity instead.

"I'm sure, so sure," I say, letting my arms land like dead weight on the bed, the cheap fabric rough against my skin.

"All right."

When I feel the bed dip between my legs, I instinctively open them for him and watch as he brings a condom package to his mouth. As he rips it open with his teeth, I admire his perfect full lips that emphasize how good-looking he is.

I feel pleased with myself.

So fucking pleased because he wants me.

Mr. Callahan wants me. Me. Can you believe it? Chubby Blaire. Ugly and awkward Blaire.

Unlovable Blaire.

I guess I'm not that ugly anymore. My body? What was considered fat as a child is now called boobs and ass. Guys want it. They want me. They want to touch me, grope me, feel me … they want to screw me. And it feels good to be wanted … so good. It makes me feel powerful, and like a potent drug spreading inside your bloodstream, I want more.

I need more.

"Hurry up," I say, not bothering to be shy or coy about it. I mean, he brought me here to have sex, right?

"Fuck, give me a second, Blaire. Trying to get the damn condom on my dick."

As he rolls the rubber down his hard shaft, his eyes wander over my bare chest, my face, my spread legs. Shaking his head as if trying to clear his mind, he mutters, "You're so beautiful. I want you so much."

That's not the first time I've heard those words come out of a man's mouth. Josh tells me all the time how beautiful I am, how perfect I am, how much he wants me. But he's just a guy I randomly make out with. The words kind of lose their meaning when it's the same person saying them to you over and over again.

"Show me."

Those two words are all it takes for him to spread my legs wider with his hands and finally enter me. Pain shoots through my body, and a groan escapes my mouth when he covers my body with his. I feel his whole length inside me in one deep thrust.

"Christ, you're so tight."

He lifts both my legs, wrapping them around his lean waist and starts to thrust. Hard. It hurts. But I like the pain. It sobers me.

"Oh God … I love you, Blaire. I love you … I love you …'" he pants in my ear.

And that's when reality comes crashing down on me. It hits me with the speed and blinding power of a torpedo, making me realize what I'm doing. What I'm giving away. And the man doesn't even know it.

What the hell am I doing?

Proving that you are your mother's daughter.

Making her proud.

The room is filled with the noises of the man grunting his pleasure and the wet slapping of our skin; it makes me want to gag. I want to throw up. Maybe it's the alcohol I drank.

Maybe it's self-disgust.

The initial pain is gone and now I just feel sore. And strange, like an out of body experience.

He lowers his face, his lips about to connect with mine, and I feel the bile rise inside my throat. I turn my face to the side, his kiss landing on my cheek. My eyes watch the way the lights in the bathroom illuminate all its used and dirty ugliness.

"Oh God, I'm going to come … I'm going to come … I'm going to come," he continues to pant in my ear, pumping in and out of my body. Before I know what's happening, he half screams and half groans, his body going tense on top of mine.

And just like that it's over. In less than five minutes I've managed to kill a part of me.

Our breathing evens and he pulls out, moving to stand up. I push myself up on my elbows to see him inspect his condom. It still glistens. By the time he lifts his eyes, connecting with mine, I've already wrapped my body with the duvet cover.

Confusion, shock, and pleasure reflect in those brown eyes. "I—I didn't know … I …" His hands go to his hair as we stare at each other. "I didn't know you were a virgin."

easy **virtue**.

I shrug my shoulder carelessly, causing the duvet to slide down, exposing my bare breasts to him. His eyes immediately flare with lust. "It doesn't matter ... I wanted it to be you."

And that's the truth.

"But—"

"But nothing. If it bothers you, then forget it happened. I already did," I say, ending the conversation.

This is my body. I will have the last word. Not him. Not anyone. This is my life. This is my decision.

Without giving myself a chance to doubt my next words, I turn to look at him in all his naked beauty, the gold wedding ring on his finger catching my attention. "Don't worry, Mr. Callahan ... I won't tell your daughter that you fucked her classmate."

And with that, I seal my destiny.

chapter two.

I DIDN'T HAVE AN ABUSIVE CHILDHOOD. My parents didn't beat me, didn't yell at me—they just weren't there. I was the lonely child who talked to her animals and dolls. But in my case, the absence didn't make the heart grow fonder. With time, and after many tears shed and unheard prayers to a deaf God, absence made my heart grow bitter and hard. It froze me from the inside out.

I didn't have love, but I never lacked beautiful things without a heartbeat.

My parents gave me gifts, not love ... or was it their love that was offered with each tangible gift?

Maybe those *things* were just substitutes for their love and their presence.

Maybe that's why I associate happiness with possessions?

As a child, I didn't hunger for any of those things. I hungered for the love of my parents. For a motherly caress or a sweet pat on the shoulder as they told me that they were proud of me. I longed for a tender embrace in my darkest hours ...

But I had nothing.

I was nothing.

I'm still nothing.

And I don't care anymore.

That chubby girl who cried herself to sleep every night … the same girl who kneeled by her bed and prayed to the skies above for a happy family—for someone to *see* her …

That chubby girl is gone forever.

And in her stead is me—beautiful, shiny, *empty* Blaire. Attention-loving Blaire. Really, after so many years without anyone noticing me, I now thrive on the feeling I get when all eyes are on me. Men or women, I don't care as long as they see me. As long as they follow me whenever I step into a room.

I'm in the midst of rolling the waistband of my plaid skirt to make it shorter when I hear the soft vibration of my phone. Walking away from the tall mahogany dresser, I make my way to the bed where my phone is lying amongst a pile of yellow fluffy pillows. Throwing myself on the bed, I feel the mattress bounce underneath me and smile when I see the name of the caller.

Mr. Callahan.

Just because I feel like fucking around with his mind, I wait to answer for a couple more rings.

"Hi, Matthew." Mr. Callahan's name feels like a dirty secret on my lips.

"Hello, Blaire … I thought you weren't going to answer," he teases.

"Maybe …"

"You little tease. Can you sneak out of school during your lunch hour? My schedule cleared up for the afternoon, and I want to see you again."

I bite my lip and rub my legs together; the soreness is gone since a week has already passed. I picture us back in the same seedy motel room with its dirty yellow-colored curtains and avocado furniture, and the memory alone makes the smells of his sweat and the moldy rug fill my nose once more. It would be nice to meet at a respectable hotel in town instead of our usual place, but keeping our affair anonymous is paramount for him.

"Tut-tut," I say. "Asking a senior in high school to skip school, Matthew?"

He chuckles. "It's the only time I'll be able to see you and be alone with you until next week. Besides, I bought you something that I think you might like."

"Oh, yeah? What did you get me?"

"Well, if you want to find out you'll have to come and meet me."

I giggle like the seventeen-year-old girl that I am. "Matthew! Please tell me!"

"I knew I'd be able to find your weakness … so you like presents, huh?"

"Not usually, but I guess I do now."

He chuckles once more. "Send me a picture of yourself and I'll tell you what it is."

"What kind of picture do you want?" I ask flirtatiously.

"Whatever you want to send me, Blaire. I just want to see your pretty face—I miss you," he says, his voice growing deeper.

His words sink in my head, the real meaning hidden between the lines. I can almost picture him sitting in his office chair behind the desk looking pristine in his silvery-grey suit, waiting to jerk off to anything I send him.

"Okay," I whisper.

"Good … I'll be waiting."

After I hang up, I continue to lie on my bed and stare at my light-blue ceiling while my fingers play with my cellphone. I wonder briefly why it feels like I'm selling my soul, but I dismiss the thought as quickly as it comes.

Shimmying out of my skirt, the waistband touching my skin as it goes down, I'm left wearing only my white shirt and navy blue vest and a pair of white cotton panties. I open the camera application on my phone and lift an arm in the air so I can take a picture of myself lying on the bed.

I can feel some loose wisps of hair tickling my chin as I lower my hand and place it inside my underwear. My heartbeat accelerates in anticipation and my breath shortens as I begin to rub myself slowly, imagining the soft, wet caress of his tongue inside me, licking, lapping ... fucking me.

My cheeks burn a rosy pink as I feel my lips swell. Closer. Much closer. A moan escapes and I'm there, snapping a picture for Mr. Callahan at the same time my body floats high on ecstasy and bright colors twirl in my head.

There ... that should do.

Once I'm satisfied with the shot—a shot that showcases a voluptuous girl with hair the color of coal and skin as pale as the moonlight, touching herself for her lover on a bed covered in daisies, her blue eyes sparkling with a feverish light that promises the forbidden—I send it. Not a minute goes by before I receive a text message from him. When the image has fully loaded, a tarnished smile touches my lips as I stare at the ice-blue box wrapped in an elaborate white bow.

Maybe that voice inside my head wasn't wrong after all.

I *am* selling my soul.

And the sad part is ...

I don't care.

I'm walking through the halls of my high school with my back erect and my chin held high like a regal queen. Fear of my classmates' scorn is pushed so far back in the recesses of my heart that I've almost forgotten it exists—almost—but the slight tremble in my hands tells me otherwise. *Fuck.*

Looking around, but not making eye contact with anyone, I sense the way crowds open to let me through as if I'm some animal carrying a contagious disease. Or maybe it's because they just want to get a better look at my ass in my short plaid skirt. Same difference if you ask me because I don't mind either—I enjoy both.

There are no girlfriends waiting for me by my locker with a ready smile on their faces and today's gossip on the tips of their tongues. No best friend about to link her arm with mine as we make our way to first period English while chatting about our weekend and boys. There's no one ... at least no one that counts.

Growing up in a home with no siblings and self-absorbed parents was a lonely way to live life for a child. However, loneliness taught me to be comfortable being alone ... *or maybe it just hardened me?*

It was the same way in school, too—it still is. I have no friends. It all goes back to the day I found out the reason no one wanted to be friends with me.

We were only nine years old.

It was lunchtime on a cool spring day. The sun was warm on my skin, but the air still sent a chill running through my body. I was making my way to an empty bench far away from the playground when I saw Paige and her posse approaching me. It was too late to avoid them. I remember lowering my eyes to the ground, pretending that I didn't see them and hoping to get them to ignore me, but I wasn't that lucky. As soon as I was close enough, I heard Paige, who was flawless, say to her friends, "She's so fat. I wonder if she eats in her sleep." There was snickering and then someone added, "Did you know that her mom left her and her dad for another man when she was like two years old but then came back? My mom told me to never be friends with her because her mom steals daddies, and her dad is always drunk."

11

I felt my heart skip a beat as my chest contracted with pain and tears blurred my eyes. With each word, they killed me a little bit more. Then Paige added, "Oh yeah, I heard my mom talking to my daddy about it. She also said that her dad came to a meeting with scratches all over his neck and face and smelling like alcohol." She paused. "Anyway, she told me to never be friends with her. I wanted to tell her that she didn't have to worry because I would never be friends with a girl who looks like a fat duck."

They burst out laughing, and when they saw me stop and stare at them as tears fell down my cheeks, they began to laugh louder and harder until their cruel delight was all I could hear.

I began to run away from them as fast as I could, but the ringing in my ears and the ache in my chest wouldn't stop. Their harsh words wouldn't let me escape my ugly reality.

It all made sense after that. Hearing them talk had brought back memories of all the crying, fighting and yelling. When she mentioned my dad's wounds, it reminded me of that night, and the horror I'd felt seeing my parents in one of the lowest points in their marriage. I remembered the courage it took that little girl, not even eight years old, to stand between them, and beg them to stop fighting and love each other, just as she loved them both. The tears streamed down her face, and her voice shook with pain.

Suddenly, I understood why their parents wouldn't allow them to come whenever I invited the pretty and popular girls for sleepovers. I understood why my mother, who was the prettiest amongst all the moms, had no friends. And I understood why my classmates' fathers always seemed to stare at her like she was something shiny and beautiful to look at. I understood why my nanny, the only person who truly loved me and didn't find me an annoyance, said that my father had been a good man, a brilliant man. A man who, when left with nothing, battled ghosts with the only weapons available to him—hatred and alcohol.

That day, with Paige's cruel words still spinning in my head like a tornado, leaving total wreckage in their wake, I grew up and kissed my childhood good-bye.

After that day, I discovered one indelible truth. I discovered that love wasn't everything that mattered in life. It was an emotion that not many had the luxury of feeling without any pain attached to it.

Many say that love will set you free, but I disagree … love is a cage, a very painful one; its gilded bars made with yearning, heartache, and unfulfilled dreams. And the moment I realized that love wasn't necessary to one's survival I became free. No one would have the power to hurt me again.

That realization set me free.

If love had been enough, the love I had given my parents would have been enough for them. Enough for them to want to love me back. Enough for them to want to give our family a chance. Just *enough*.

But you know what? You can wish in one hand and shit in the other.

So I said, "Fuck them."

I stopped caring; I didn't want to care anymore.

I made a decision that no one—*no one*—was ever going to hurt me like they did. And whatever was left of my heart, I surrounded it with so many thorns and spikes that if you ever came anywhere near it, I would willingly and happily hurt you.

This was the new me.

And then I got pretty—beautiful, really—and shed all the baby weight from my younger years. Like the ugly duckling from my favorite childhood story, I turned into a swan. Though beautiful on the outside, I felt ugly, so very ugly on the inside.

Men of all ages started to hit on me—their attention making me feel high and powerful. A delectable feeling came over me whenever I saw a man's cock get hard as he looked at my ass, probably picturing himself fucking me, or saw the hunger in his eyes. It made me wet.

Which explains why I gave my virginity away to Mr. Matthew Callahan. I chose him deliberately, and trust me when I say that my heart had nothing to do with my decision. He was the father of the girl who made my life miserable growing up after all. *And maybe I chose him for that exact reason.*

After "bumping" into each other at the coffee shop multiple times, it became obvious that we both kept going back to see each other. Flirty comments were exchanged, each pushing the envelope of what was right further and further away until we crossed the line unequivocally. The first time, he fingered me as we made out in the backseat of his expensive car while he told me about the many times he had imagined himself doing this.

The second time we had sex that first night, he came inside my body, panting how lovely and perfect I was. As I felt him shake above me, I remember thinking that this was the same man who I'd wished so many times to be my own father. The love and adoration he showed his family was perfection.

What a joke, right?

The paragon of our town had just fucked the shit out of a seventeen-year-old, doggy-style, in a seedy motel an hour away from his house, while his daughter and wife went to a tea function ...

I'm a couple of lockers away from mine when Josh intercepts me. Hot and popular Josh. Every girl wants him and every guy wants to be him. He's the benchmark for perfection, captain of every sport that matters. He is *the* guy in our high school.

He grabs me by the waist, saying, "Sup, baby? Wanna meet me after school and go for a drive?" He leans closer and whispers in my ear, his hot breath kissing the exposed skin of my neck. "I miss your sweet little mouth."

Feeling my skin burn with shame, and maybe excitement, I push him away. "Forget about it, Josh. I can't today … I'm busy." Of course, I don't add that I'll be busy collecting a gift from Mr. Callahan.

"What the fuck? You've been giving me that bullshit excuse for the past month!" he exclaims, anger and confusion marring his boyish beauty.

Sounds about right. I believe that's how long Mr. Callahan and I have been seeing each other in secret.

He pins me with his angry, hurt gaze. "Are you seeing someone else?"

I flip my hair carelessly, not missing the way his eyes land on my boobs. "Whatever, Josh. Stop being so immature … I gotta go or I'm going to be late to class." I move away from him and begin to walk toward my locker.

"You're such a bitch, you know? I don't know why I waste my time with you when I could have anyone I want."

I turn around and face him once more, half smiling, half mocking him. "Because I'm worth it, and you know it."

Not wanting to hear what he has to say next, I leave him standing frozen in place with an incredulous expression on his face and begin to walk once more. Out of the corner of my eye, I notice a large crowd has gathered around Josh and me. Maybe they decided I was not contagious enough, or maybe they just wanted to hear our exchange. *Whatever. It's not like they don't already know my dirty laundry.*

I'm walking past Paige when I see her scrunching up her nose at me as if I smell like something putrid. I taunt her with a smile while she rolls her eyes and says, "As if," to her friends. Then I hear her say to the same group of bullies who once pulled my chair out right as I was sitting down, causing me to fall on my ass, "I can't understand why guys find her so attractive when her mouth looks like it has been punched because her lips are so big."

Smiling to myself like the cat that ate the cream, I wonder what she would think if she knew how much her dad likes having those lips wrapped around his cock.

He hasn't complained.

chapter three

Months later...

IN THE SAME MOTEL ROOM that has become a second home to me, where the smell of mold buried in the green rug has grown to be soothing and comforting like its color, the rough sheets on the bed familiar on my skin, I say good-bye to my first lover, to my benefactor, to a man I've grown to care for. *But I guess not really since I'm leaving him anyway.*

"Please don't go to New York City. Stay with me ... I need you," a naked Mr. Callahan begs on his knees, his arms wrapped around my waist and his face buried in my equally naked and flat stomach.

With the aroma of sweat and sex still floating in the air and the lingering taste of his semen on my tongue, I observe how a grown man who I've admired for his power and influence in this small town turns into a child at my feet. I want to push him away, but instead I let my hands settle on top of his head, splaying my fingers in his soft brown hair. "I can't, Matthew ... I can't continue living under the same roof as my mother. I want to get out of this town."

Soon after I started sleeping with Mr. Callahan, my parents got divorced. Not that it came as a surprise to anyone, especially me. They didn't really care what happened to me. My dad said I needed to be with my mom, and my mom said I needed to be with my dad. At the end of the day, I ended up living with my mom—but only because she got the house. However, in a week I turn eighteen and I'll leave this town with all of its ugly and bitter memories and never turn back.

"Don't ... if you need a place to live, let me get you an apartment. I'll pay for it—I'll pay for everything—anything you want. I'll give you the life you've always wanted," he says, bringing me back to this moment.

"How different would that arrangement be from what we have going on, Matthew? You already pay for everything I own."

And it's true. As a child, I didn't want toys—I wanted the love of my parents. But during my time fucking Paige's dad, I've discovered the seductive power of money, of having someone support me and buy me all the nice things I want for sex in return. With Mr. Callahan in my life, there was no need for my parents—he helped me to finally cut the "umbilical cord." Mr. Callahan gave me that and more just for regular head in the backseat of his Audi while his wife thought he was at work. His money and protection have shown me how independent I can be just by spreading my legs.

"I don't know, Blaire ... I don't know ... please don't leave me. I love you," he says, his breath hitting my skin. "I love you, Blaire," he repeats as he begins to kiss my stomach and every part of me his lips can touch, inhaling me.

I lift my eyes and stare at my reflection in the smudged mirror above the bed, observing how empty my eyes look—like bottomless pits filled with nothing.

Nothing.

"If you love me as you say, you need to let me go. I need to get out of this place …"

"But what about me? What about us? Is it because I'm married?"

I laugh, and the sound is chilling even to my own ears. "I don't think it matters, Matthew. I've already made up my mind and nothing you say will change it."

He lets go of me and stands up. The big, wide shoulders that I've seen so many times shaking with mirth, or supporting my legs as he goes down on me, hang in defeat. "One day, you're going to fall in love with a man and I hope he breaks your heart, Blaire. When that happens, you'll know what kind of pain you're capable of inflicting, and maybe then you'll grow a heart and hopefully find your humanity."

I want to say that I doubt it, but I remain silent. Sometimes silence speaks louder than words, and I have nothing left for him. "I'm sorry for hurting you, Matthew, but I thought you knew, like me, that this wasn't going to last forever."

Overcome with feeling, Matthew doesn't reply but simply shakes his head as he takes one last look at me and then makes his way to the bathroom.

With the sound of the shower running in the background, I get dressed. As the black cotton of my dress flows down my body, I allow myself to think of Mr. Callahan one last time. The memory of the way he looked at me before he disappeared in the bathroom makes my heart contract, so I apologize to him wordlessly for causing him pain and hope that one day he forgives me. I'm not worthy, and one day he will see that too.

When I'm ready to leave, I take one last look at the seedy place, but instead of trying to engrave its look in my head, I pour all my memories back into this room. I'm not taking anything with me: not one smile, not one kiss, not one memento. I don't want them. I don't have any need for them. What I am taking is everything you can put a price on, everything that I care for, everything that won't hurt me—all the gifts and money he showered me with.

And isn't money what makes the world go round?

As I'm closing the door behind me, a small thought crosses my mind that maybe I'm more fond of Mr. Callahan than I care to admit. But in the end, it doesn't matter.

Once upon a time there was an unloved young Blaire, who made a promise to an empty room with only her stuffed animals and her dog as witnesses. She promised that she would never let herself grow close to anyone; that she would never let love cut her wings and make a prisoner of her once again. That way she would remain safe and unharmed.

Well, it is time for me to fulfill that promise I made so long ago.

One week later…

I'm packing my red suitcase, grabbing every single item of silk, cotton, lace, and leather I have paid for with my body, when my mom walks into my bedroom.

"What are you doing?" she asks, her perfect golden hair looking like a million bucks.

I don't bother acknowledging her, instead, I reach over my suitcase to grab Winkler, my old grey teddy bear, and put him next to a Louis Vuitton bag that Mr. Callahan bought for me.

She comes to stand next to me and grabs me by the arm so we're looking at each other. "Answer me when I'm speaking to you, Blaire. Where are your manners?"

I pull my arm free of her hold as her nails leave a burning trace on my skin. "What does it look like I'm doing? I'm packing my shit and leaving this fucking town."

"Watch your mouth, Blaire. I'm your mother," she replies bitingly.

I snort. "Are you? I wouldn't have known."

It happens before I even see it coming. The first physical touch in at least eight years from my mom is not a hug or a caress ... no. It's a slap across my face.

How fitting.

My hand instantly covers the sore spot where she hit me. I rub my cheek, trying to soothe the sting of her palm as it spreads heat across my skin.

"How dare you," she breathes.

"How dare I what? Speak the truth?" A destructive smile sweeps across my face. It feels good. "You know what? Don't bother. I'm out, and I'm never coming back. And aren't you glad?" I look her up and down, noticing the expensive clothes she's wearing. The clothes she couldn't have afforded. The clothes another man must have paid for. "After all you've never cared about me."

My mother doesn't even bat an eyelash. "And how do you expect to pay for this? You don't even have a job."

I laugh in her face. "Well ... how does that saying go? Oh yes, I remember now." I tap my forehead as if a bright idea has just occurred to me. "The apple doesn't fall far from the tree, right? I guess in our case that holds true." I start packing again. My flight leaves in four hours and I have no intention of missing it.

After some silence, I assume she's already left my room when her answer comes echoing through the air. "Don't think too highly of yourself, Blaire. Your looks will fade ... and you'll be all alone."

I close my suitcase, hearing it click shut, then lift it off the bed and put it down on the floor next to me. After I grab my bag and put Winkler and my old paperback of *Persuasion* in it, I'm able to finally stare her in the eye. "Just like you, right?"

"How dare—"

"Don't bother." I reach for the handle of my suitcase and head toward the door, my shoulder bumping against hers as I walk past her. "I'll be smart just like you, *Mom*. I'll make you proud, I promise," I spit.

As I walk out of my mother's house, filling my lungs with clean air, a sense of freedom washes over me. And right now, while I take my first steps into the unknown, I realize that there's nothing holding me back. Nothing. This is my chance to shape myself into the woman I want to be without gossip following my every step, or memories shining like neon lights on every corner with every item I see.

So here and now is where my story begins. My tale. Will it be a love story or a tragedy? Maybe it will be a farce. Who the fuck knows, really. Only time will tell, but I can already see it written…

On a breezy summer morning when the birds sang their beautiful love songs and the sun shone brightly in the cloudless sky above, Blaire White turned eighteen years old. She left her old and forsaken town in search of the American Dream—a big fat wallet filled with lots of green dollars.

And why the hell not? With my body and looks, I *will* conquer the world.

It's my destiny.

part two.
easy virtue
present

chapter four.

I am beautiful.
I am beautiful.
I am beautiful.

STANDING NAKED IN FRONT OF A MIRROR, I look at my reflection while chanting the litany my brain is trying to engrave in my heart. It isn't working. Nothing ever works. I don't believe it. I never will. Instead, my heart keeps telling my mind over and over again ...

You are not beautiful. Look at you. You are worthless. You are unlovable. Not even your parents loved you.

But *I am* looking at myself, and what I see is breathtaking.

It has to be.

The admiration that follows me everywhere I go testifies to that fact. If only I could remove all traces of those childhood memories that constantly crowd my mind, reminding me how unworthy of love I am. If I could, then I know I could make myself believe what my brain has been telling me all along. I know I could make myself believe the words that countless of men have whispered in my ear while they were inside of me.

Lifting my fingertips to touch my face, I trace the soft angles of my chin, the curve of my winged eyebrows, the shape of my high cheekbones. The way the outer corners of my almond-shaped eyes lift gives me a feline look. The face I see belongs to a beautiful, almost too beautiful girl.

I smile into the mirror as I begin to trace my body with my hand. The hand travels a path from my shoulder down to my breasts, caressing the rosy tips, and then it continues down to my smooth stomach. I can't help but wonder if this is all I'm about.

Is this everything I'm worth—a body and a face?

A voice inside my head tells me that things could be different if only I'd allow it, but I ignore it. Instead, I take one last glance at my naked body and walk toward my closet, looking for an outfit to wear tonight.

It's been five years since I moved to New York City and in those years I've managed to live a life full of clichés. I've become a walking cliché, but I don't mind because at least I can say that I'm living and experiencing life. I've been a waitress, a receptionist, a sales representative in a department store ... I even tried acting school for the hell of it. And through it all, I've managed to keep my heart intact and my feelings at bay.

Looking around at my expensively furnished apartment—my borrowed dream—I'm surrounded by glamour and false security. A white bedspread and headboard, a white rug, a white night table, white candles, white lamps, and blocks of white canvas as the only thing adorning my lavender walls. White. White. White. I breathe white. I breathe the color of innocence. Yet this place couldn't be more soiled than the color black.

I shake my head and focus on getting ready for my date tonight with Walker.

Walker Woodsmith Jr.—the name alone drips with money. With his blond hair, sky blue eyes, body of an Olympic swimmer, a pedigree similar to the Kennedys, and the swagger of Jay-Z—he is God reincarnated. And he fucks like one too. It feels as though he brings me closer to God every time he plays my body like a perfectly tuned instrument.

Just thinking about him makes my heart rate rise. With Walker, everything is always fast, angry, hard, painful.

And I love it.

Once I finish applying the last coat of dark red to my lips, I take two steps away from the bathroom counter so I can take a better look at myself. I smile at my flawless reflection in the mirror. Rivers of straight black hair, skin that has never been kissed by the sun, eyes the color of bluebells, and an hourglass figure. This Blaire won't be bullied by the cool kids in school. This Blaire won't be ignored.

This Blaire will shine.

Satisfied with the way the little black lacy, see-through dress I'm wearing molds to my curves, the thin layer of lace showing the paleness of my skin, I decide this will do. I look sinful. I look like sex—and that's what I'm selling. I want men to want me. I want women to be jealous of me. I *need* to feel desired.

After slipping my feet into a killer pair of black Miu Miu stilettos (and by killer I mean they are as gorgeous as they are painful), I grab a sparkly clutch encrusted with crystals and head out the door.

Standing on the corner outside my building, relishing in the attention I seem to be attracting, I lift an arm, feeling the golden bangles I'm wearing slide down my wrist, and flag a cab. As I wait for one to stop, I look around me, admiring the way the city comes alive when darkness has fallen upon us. It's not like it doesn't feel the same way during the day—it's different—better. As night takes over, there's a wild frenzy of excitement and licentious behavior that runs deep through the streets of Manhattan, swiping away with it all of its inhabitants. And as I swim in those turbulent waters, my body packed with energy, I've never felt freer.

I'm watching a couple hold hands as they walk their dog across the street when I hear my phone ring. I open my small clutch and reach for the white rectangle that holds my entire life in its minuscule memory chip. I smile when I see the picture of my best friend—the only person who knows the real me.

"Yo," I answer. We like to pretend that we can talk all cool, but we're pretty lame at it if we're being honest with ourselves.

"Sup, lady?" she answers.

A cab finally stops in front of me. "One sec, Elly." I grab the handle and pull the door open. Once I glide to the middle of the backseat, feeling the coolness of the leather underneath me rub against my bare skin, I give the address to the cab driver and go back to my conversation.

"Back, sorry about that. Anyway, how are you, stranger? I feel like I haven't spoken to you in ages."

Elly laughs. "That's because you've been too busy sucking Walker and his wallet dry."

I smile. "You're correct ... on both accounts."

My answer makes her laugh once more. "You're shameless, Blaire, but that's why I love you. And as long as he treats my girl right, I don't care if he's a pompous ass."

"You know he does, and I thought he grew on you?" I want to add that even if he didn't treat me right, I'd stay with him by choice, but I don't.

I'm very attracted to Walker—his cock is a religious experience, and he's the kind of guy who men respect and women dream about. He's filthy rich, and we have a lot of fun and wild times together. But here's the thing ... as horrible as it sounds, I wouldn't give him the time of day if I knew he was broke and a nobody. I may not believe in love, but I do believe in practicality and goals. I don't want to live comfortably—I want luxury. I want an easy life. And a broke guy would never be able to offer all those expensive things to me.

It all comes down to priorities. And a faux happy marriage to the man I love, two point five kids, with a moderately sized Victorian house in the suburbs doesn't make the top of my list. Because what they fail to show you in the catalog of life is that behind those walls, the couple will eventually fall out of love and become strangers. The mom will grow tired of taking care of her kids and of her mundane life, growing anxious as she wonders if looking at a pile of folded clothes is all the excitement left in her life. The father will grow bored of fucking the same woman over and over again. Maybe he'll grow frustrated and dissatisfied with his life and turn to alcohol instead of another woman. Or maybe he'll grow resentful of what he has to give up in order to provide for his family. And what about those two point five kids who look so happy in the glossy pages of said catalog? Behind those pretty smiles are hidden tears of neglect, laughless hearts, and days upon days of loneliness.

And that is not my dream.

So am I calculating? Yes, completely. I'm a gold digger, but I'm also smart. Love fades … or it's selfish … or unkind … but a diamond? A diamond will last forever.

And because I'm a cynical bitch, I'm very aware that I need to capitalize on my looks while I still have them because those will fade as well.

"I guess I still don't trust him fully," I hear Elly say. "I wish you could just settle with a nice guy who loves you for who you are and not what you look like."

I laugh as I stare out the window, watching the cab picking up speed, people and street lights blending together. "If they

easy **virtue**.

knew the real me, they would run for the hills, Elly. Come on, let's be honest here."

After a moment of silence, she replies, "Not if they knew the *real* you. The one you try so hard to hide. May I remind you what you did for me?"

"Blah, stop it. But seriously, I can't believe you're still iffy about Walker. We're good together. Anyway, tell me, how was your vacation?" Elly was away for two weeks visiting family in California.

She huffs. "Don't go changing the subject on me, Blaire. And I don't know … there's just something about Walker that throws me off."

"I think you're thinking too much into it. We're just having fun."

And we are.

I was the pretty hostess of Homme, an upscale restaurant in Midtown that Walker and his friends used to frequent around lunch hour when we met. At first, he only saw me as a nice piece of ass to spend a couple of hours with whenever he felt like it (and maybe he still does—who knows). I saw the expensive suit, the even more expensive watch, and when I heard his last name, my panties almost fell down to the ground. He was like the long lost City of Atlantis for girls like me.

The click and clack of utensils and the buzz of chatter filled my ears as I stood in my booth by the front of the restaurant, I preened like a peacock for Walker.

First stolen glance.

I felt my skin tingle.

Second stolen glance.

I felt my skin grow hot.

Third stolen glance.

I was burning.

Our eyes continued to connect over and over again—we couldn't stop.

By the time his bill was paid, I'd thought he was going to stop by the front and ask me for my number like so many other men before him had. But he hadn't. As a matter of fact, as he crossed the small space between the metal booth where I was standing and the large glass doors, he didn't even glance my way. I watched his perfectly combed blond hair shine like burnt gold in the sun as he stepped into the street. When I heard the roar of his laughter at something his friend must have said, I felt it vibrate in my bones.

And then he was gone.

I wish I could say that I didn't care and that the moment he walked out the door he walked out of my mind. But it would be a lie. He remained in my thoughts for the rest of the day. When my shift was over, I kissed my coworkers on the cheek goodbye, grabbed my coat and headed out the door.

I felt my heart stop beating as soon as I saw him.

Walker.

Reclined against his black BMW parked across the street from the restaurant staring straight at me. His sleek hair parted to the side in a way that should have been obnoxious, but on him it totally worked. A confident smile graced his face. It was the kind of smile that only those born in privilege and to whom the word "no" is nonexistent have. He looked gorgeous. And the slut in me instantly wondered what it would feel like to run my hands through his long hair as I rode him like a mechanical bull.

I watched him cross the street, walking in my direction. When he was standing in front of me, he simply said, "Go out with me."

I wanted to say yes.

easy **virtue.**

But I knew that if I wanted him to treat me differently, to give me everything I wanted and to want me more than any other pretty face he could have, I needed to make him work for it. I needed to make him work for my attention. *Isn't the chase always better than the catch?* Guys like him thrive on it.

So I gave him my best smile—a smile that said yes with the eyes but no with the tongue. "No, I'm sorry but I'm busy tonight and I don't even know you."

He grinned, his eyes sparkling with a devious light. "Somehow I had the feeling that you were going to say no."

I ran a hand through my long hair seductively, watching him follow my movements. "Smart man. Anyway, I've got to go—"

"Walker. The name is Walker."

I turned around and started to walk away. "See you around, Walker."

I was almost halfway down the street when I heard him yell after me, "I won't take no for an answer, you know."

I stopped and turned around to face him, my hands on my hips. "Oh really?" I felt my toes curl inside my expensive Mary Jane pumps and my heart rate accelerate as I waited for his answer. *See ... the chase is always so much better.*

An easy and slow smile appeared on his face, making him look like the cocky bastard that he was, but I loved it. "You'll give me another chance. You'll see. And then ..."

"And then what?"

"I guess you'll just have to find out."

And that was it. He turned around, waited until there was a clear gap in the traffic, then crossed the street, got in his car and drove away. I watched him speed into the sunset as people walked past me.

I said "no" several times after that, but Walker never gave up. Never. If anything, he'd pursued me more aggressively and single-mindedly than ever before. As with all good things in life, he knew I was worth it. And somehow he also knew that the way to my heart was money—gifts, expensive dinners, a better apartment …

He gave me everything.

chapter five.

WITH CHAMPAGNE AND CAVIAR INUNDATING my every sense, I slither through the light wooden floors of the Lila Acheson Wallace Wing in The Met. As I walk, I pretend to admire the expensive jewelry being showcased tonight by a famous designer whose name I can't remember. A multicolored diamond butterfly sparkles to my left and a cobra made out of black stones glistens to my right. Rows upon rows of precious gems twinkle under the soft lights of the room, flooding the space between the walls with the glow of a thousand stars. Furtive glances. Secrets gossiped. Beauty criticized. Lofty music fills the atmosphere as the über rich mingle and pretend to like each other, yet you can almost taste their conceit and derision for one another in the air.

This is Walker's world, and I love it.

Standing across the room, where the crowd is thinner and the music fainter, I spot Walker's blond head in the corner of the room, talking to a group of his colleagues and their wives. He looks polished and worth every penny of his trust fund in his sleek black tuxedo, perfectly starched white shirt and black bowtie. His long golden hair parted to the side shines like the sun. He is truly flawless.

I smile because it's hard to picture that this is the same guy who likes to snort coke off my tits as he fucks me while hardcore porn plays in the background. He looks untouchable and so cool, but his searching eyes, scanning the crowd for me give him up. He's wondering where I am. *He did tell me not to go too far, after all.* Soon after we arrived at the party, I gave him some space to talk to his friends and do his thing while I did mine. I hate clingy people, so I avoid being one.

I grab a third flute of champagne from a passing waiter, and try to decide which of the different displays to check out first when my eyes land on a spectacular piece of jewelry. On a bed of black silk, similar to my hair color, lies an extravagant necklace made of diamonds and rubies—a small heaven within one's reach as long as you can afford the price.

I bridge the space between the glass protecting the necklace and me until it's within my reach, fighting the urge to touch the cool surface. As if under a spell, I observe how the rows of diamonds embedded in platinum form leaves and thorns. At its center is a rose made out of red diamonds almost as big as my palm.

I feel someone walk up and stand next to me, but I don't give him or her a second thought as I continue to admire the way the light hits the gems, making them shine.

"Beautiful, isn't it?"

His voice is smooth and commanding, dripping absolute power. I keep my eyes locked on the display. Call it sixth sense, but somehow I know that under no circumstance should I make eye contact with the stranger who speaks like the ruler of the world.

"Yes," I say simply.

"I wonder how much it is?" the man asks.

"I don't think it matters … I highly doubt anyone can afford it."

He chuckles, and the sound is more delicious than his voice. Lusher. "Oh, but I can."

35

I smile at his self-assurance. *I love cocky assholes.* "I still doubt it."

"You shouldn't. I only speak the truth," he retorts coolly. His voice is nonchalant yet his words leave no room for disbelief—a demand and a statement all in one.

Suddenly, the noises of the room become distant. People talking and laughing amongst friends and the orchestra playing all fade away until all I hear is him speaking.

And at this moment, that is all that matters.

"The truth is very subjective, *sir.*"

"The truth may be subjective but money isn't. Money can buy anything."

His answer is like an electroshock, jumpstarting my brain from a champagne-induced haze. My pulse begins to accelerate, excitement making it hard to take a deep breath. *Don't look at him … don't.*

"Oh really," I say, my voice dripping with sarcasm. *He's right, though.*

"Of course. I believe everything," he pauses, "and *everyone* has a price."

Curiosity winning the battle against curiosity, I turn to face him, *and what a fucking big mistake that is.* When our eyes meet, I feel incapacitated of all sense and movement. The sight of him takes my breath away. This man gives the term "lust at first sight" a whole new meaning.

In my short twenty-three years, I've been with extremely handsome men, perfect even, but to classify the man standing next to me in any kind of category would be a disservice to him, and not really fair to the others. Longish, light brown hair wildly framing his face, vacant eyes the color of dollar bills, a slightly crooked nose, and a mouth that begs to be buried deep within your thighs. His beauty is as harsh as it is stunningly perfect. Dressed in a simple black tuxedo and unbuttoned white shirt, the man exudes innate virility and grace, reminding me of a black panther stalking his prey. And just like a panther, it's the pure raw and powerful energy emanating from within him that I find most attractive. Because just by standing next to him, I get the sense that his word is always the last spoken and his wishes the first ones to be fulfilled. He doesn't ask, he demands. He doesn't hope, he expects.

He's quiet for a moment; his uncanny eyes hold me captive as though they are baring my soul to him and I hate it. I tighten my hold on the crystal flute. I want to look away, but I can't. The way he's staring at me makes me want to squirm.

"I wonder … do *you* have one?" he asks softly before turning to examine the piece of jewelry once more.

"A what?" I ask, momentarily stunned.

He smiles. "A price."

"For the right amount … I just might," I say quietly, my heart beating so fast it feels as though it wants out of my chest. As soon as the words leave my mouth, there's no shock coursing down my body, no rolling waves of shame pulling me down for having said that to a complete stranger—nothing.

And why should there be? I am who I am.

I'm staring at his profile, waiting for him to acknowledge my answer, when a breeze of cool air floats past us, making me shiver. About to chase the goose bumps on my arm with my hand, I watch as he slowly turns to look at me, catching me staring at him. Time stands still as I watch him raise his large tanned hand and touch my bare shoulder, his fingertips lightly grazing the temporary small bumps covering it. Then he smiles as if he knows that my skin is tingling from his scalding touch, and looks away.

"I thought so."

We remain standing next to each other for another minute or so, the distance between us almost nonexistent. *It would be so easy to reach out and hold his hand.* The sound of an incoming call breaks the silence, bringing us back to reality.

He takes his cell phone out of the inner pocket of his tuxedo jacket and ignores the call after noting the name of the caller. He lifts his gaze to meet my own.

"Sorry about that."

"It's okay. I should go … I'm here with someone," I reply, not really wanting to leave him just yet.

"Yes, that's probably a good idea."

I frown. He didn't have to be quite so blunt. The stranger extends a hand toward me, holding something in his fingers.

"Here … "

I open my hand as I feel the edges of what I assume is his business card poke the skin of my palm. "What's this?" I ask stupidly.

"My business card, of course."

"Obviously … but why?"

He smiles, but it doesn't reach his eyes. "Let's just say that I'm an interested buyer."

And then he's gone.

He turns and walks away from me, disappearing into a sea of colorful gowns and black suits. As the sounds of the party infiltrate my ears once more, I lower my gaze to stare at the simple cream-colored card in my hand. Its simplistic and elegant design draws attention to the name printed in bold black letters on the paper.

Lawrence Rothschild.

I smile and let my fingertips trail his name. *It depends on what you're willing to pay, Mr. Rothschild.*

I'm still reeling from my encounter with the stranger when I spot Walker standing in the same place and with the same crowd as before. I run a hand through my hair nervously as I try to quiet the voices inside my head. *Should I go back? Will I see him again?* Afraid that I'll turn around and go in search of Mr. Rothschild because, let's face it, I'm fickle, I decide to join Walker and his friends.

Eyes on me, gazes filled with admiration or disapproval, it doesn't matter one way or another—I'm untouchable. It also doesn't change the fact that they can't look away from my body exposing itself through the thin layer of lace that covers every decadent inch of pale skin.

Walker looks my way, his ice-blue eyes finding mine and darkening with ravenous desire. We smile at each other. We can't look away. We fuck each other with our eyes while filthy images of his cock and where I want it flash through my mind. Dirty, so dirty. Gradually, I observe a smug smile as mouthwatering as the sweetest of sins spread across his face and it makes me feel like I'm flying. Yet, as I close the distance between us … as the buzzing of voices gets louder in my ears … as I grow wet with the promise of his taste on my tongue …

I decide not to throw Mr. Rothschild's business card away.

One never knows when it will be time for an upgrade.

I stand next to Walker, his hand reaching out for mine, linking our fingers and pulling me closer to him. Lowering his mouth to my bare shoulder, he lets his breath hit my skin before kissing it.

"I was beginning to wonder if someone stole you away," he whispers in my ear.

I glance at him sideways, a small smile playing on my lips. "I'm here, aren't I?"

"Yeah, you sure are, baby." He grins.

People cough around us. The men who saw him kiss me with familiar ownership stare at me while their partners pretend that I don't exist.

"Ugh, Walker, get a room," a female not much older than me says.

Lifting my eyes, I stare at a girl who looks eerily like me—black hair, blue eyes, pale skin but no curves. She reminds me of winter.

"Everyone, this is Bla—"

"As I was saying, Eleanor, before Walker interrupted us …" The girl turns to look the other way, talking over him without acknowledging my presence or the fact that Walker was about to introduce me to them. Her girlfriends follow suit, ignoring me as well.

Walker squeezes my hand but doesn't say a word in my defense. Suddenly feeling very small and exposed, I want to let go of him, cross my arms over my chest while I walk away and never turn back. *Maybe I'm not as untouchable as I thought.*

I'm ready to leave when, out of the corner of my eye, I see the woman named Eleanor snicker and thank God for that because it lights up an angry fire inside me. And that fire wants to burn everything and everyone in its path. I've been here before. I've been bullied, I've been purposefully ignored, I've been made fun of, but this time I won't let them win. No, I'm not that girl anymore. And maybe it's my fault because of the way I dress, or the way I let him touch me, but that doesn't give them the right to be rude to me when I barely know them. I haven't done anything to warrant their cruelty. But if she wants a reason to be a bitch to me, so be it. I'll give her and to her group of plastic friends a reason, no problem.

I let go of Walker's hold to run my hands over my hips, seemingly fixing my dress when in reality I want to draw the men's attention to the curves of my body. A taunting smirk in place, I make eye contact with Eleanor's husband. *Payback time.* He seems to have been waiting for this to happen because the moment I do, he raises his glass of champagne in salute and takes a sip, his stare unwavering. Smiling at him even though I don't feel like it, I lick my lips slowly, almost as if I could taste the bubbly liquid going down his throat on them. He seems satisfied as the usual look of greedy want glazes over his eyes, his dick likely growing hard in his tuxedo pants. He's probably the kind of man who lies down on his back and lets the woman do all the work while he pants about what a bad, bad girl she is. *Yawn.*

Satisfaction warms my bitter heart when I see the woman tugging his arm forcefully, jealousy marring her pretty features in the angry blush coating her cheeks. I chuckle. If I really wanted to screw with them, I could drop a hint to the same gentleman who's removing my clothes with his eyes and meet him in a dark corner …

But I don't. I have nothing to prove to them.

Nothing.

When I'm about to look away, Walker lets his hand land on the curve of my ass. Molding his palm like a second skin on mine, I can feel his middle finger beginning to graze the back of my thighs, slowly making its way under my skirt—closer to my hot core. The tightly packed crowd is Walker's perfect cover to his assault.

"I don't like the way Arthur is staring at you," he whispers in my ear. "At all." And then his finger is inside me.

I stare ahead of me, seeing nothing but feeling everything, and try to focus on the handsome man with black hair who happens to be holding the hand of the girl who looks like me. Walker is right. He's indeed watching me.

"He wants you," Walker whispers once again, pushing his finger all the way in. It hurts, but I love it. It sends a chill coursing up my spine, making my hand tremble as I lift a flute of champagne to my lips.

After I take a sip, I turn to look at him. "They always do."

The moment the words leave my mouth, I'm gripped by a sense of melancholy—emptiness. They all want me—my body, my face, my mouth—but none of them want *me*. None of them care to know what lies underneath it all. *There's nothing there.*

"Too bad."

Not caring that people might be staring at us and listening to our hushed conversation, he lowers his face and lets the tip his nose trace the curve of my neck before adding in a soft voice, "I want to fuck you."

Not a romantic statement, yet I can't help blushing.

Walker straightens, slowly dragging his finger out of me. "It was great catching up," he says, addressing the group, "but I'm afraid Blaire and I have to leave." He looks at me before adding, "I'm done sharing her."

More uncomfortable coughs. More angry stares. More disdain.

Less of me.

"Good night. It was great meeting you," I address the group but stare at the girls in particular.

Walker grabs my waist, ready to leave when the black-haired girl speaks. "Walker, one word before you go. Don't forget that Arthur and I are hosting a dinner party at our apartment on Tuesday to welcome back Emma from Europe," she says, smiling maliciously at me.

He tightens his hold on my waist. "I haven't forgotten. I'll be there."

Usually, I wouldn't care what he does with his time, but the way the girl is staring at me with triumph in her eyes makes a bad feeling settle in the pit of my stomach.

When we walk out of The Met, leaving that nightmare behind us, we are greeted by a dark sky illuminated with fabricated lights. The sounds of a busy night in the city crowd my ears: the angry honking of yellow cabs, hip-hop music coming from a car with its windows all the way down, a frustrated deliveryman on a bicycle ringing his bell as he tries to scatter the crowd blocking his path, the smell of Chinese food drifting out of the white plastic bags sitting behind him.

After we climb down the stairs of the museum, Walker pulls me in for a hug. With his hands wrapped around me, he lowers his mouth until his lips touch mine. Opening my mouth for him, I welcome his kiss and the delicious assault of his tongue. I wish I could say that this kiss, or any of his kisses for that matter, makes my heart sing or fills me with light, obliterating the darkness inside me, but that's not the case. I don't think it will ever happen. But his kiss makes me feel wanted, needed, yearned for. It's a kiss that doesn't ask for anything other than a physical reaction.

Twisting my hair in his hands, he gives it a tug, making me stare at him. "I—"

One moment he's gazing into my eyes and the next we're tangled in leashes and dogs while they yap and howl around us, trying to break free.

"Shit!" I hear a girl curse. "Chanel! Down girl, down!"

"What the fuck?" I hear Walker protest angrily as a huge German Shepherd stands on its hind legs, placing its paws on the lapels of Walker's pristine tuxedo, attempting to lick his face.

A giggle escapes my mouth as I watch my cool boyfriend struggling to remove the dog from his chest without any success. I'm about to help him when a black mastiff comes out of nowhere and leaps on me, the force of his jump making me lose my balance.

"Ow, ow, ow!" I exclaim, flapping my arms in the air like a duck.

My ass is close to hitting the ground when I hear a man curse. Before I make a total fool of myself by falling on the street, a firm body is behind me, breaking my fall. His arms are like corded steel bands around my waist, protecting me.

"Are you okay?" the man asks, close to my ear. The way his breath, soft and warm as a summer's breeze, hits my skin makes funny things happen inside me—of the tingly kind.

"I'm sorry. What did you say?" I ask, turning to look at him.

He chuckles. "I asked if you're all right."

Oh. *Oh.* "Oh, yeah, yes. I'm okay. I'm sorry."

I break the uncomfortable staring contest we have going on by lowering my gaze to the arms around my waist. "Your … um, your arms," I say, sounding like a total idiot. *Seriously, Blaire? Seriously?*

"What about them?" he says, tightening them.

I swallow hard, clearing my mind, and I place my hands on his to try and move them. But they won't budge. It's like they're stuck to me. "You can let go of me now."

He laughs as he releases me, the warmth of his touch gone. "My bad."

I turn to look at him and watch as the stranger smirks in a way that totally negates his apology. The small smile makes his eyes crinkle at the corners, a complete telltale. *The asshole totally liked it.*

I run a hand down my dress, smoothing it. "Thank you for—"

"Actually, don't worry about it. This has been the best part of my day."

Don't smile … don't smile …

I smile.

How could I not?

We continue to smile at each other as the angry sounds of dogs yapping and barking surround us. But then I remember Walker. Grimacing, the same thoughts seem to cross the stranger's mind right before we turn around and watch an angry looking Walker going off on the poor dog walker. She's holding the leashes to at least ten dogs, pulling and tugging in every possible direction. It's easy to see why she lost control of them.

I'm about to defend her and tell Walker to calm down, but the angry flash I see in his eyes makes me think it would be a bad idea.

"Chill, man. It's not the girl's fault that the dog jumped you," I hear the stranger say, becoming my personal hero.

I can't help but compare how different they are. With his impeccable black tuxedo, blond hair, and blue eyes, Walker seems coolly untouchable. The stranger is wearing an old looking black suit, messy brown hair that sticks up at the top, and the softest of brown eyes that seem to be as warm as the earth.

I watch as he kneels and pats some of the dogs, trying to mellow them. "There … there … calm down," he coos softly.

Walker doesn't bother answering him. He turns to look at the terrified girl. "Next time, learn how to do your job properly. It doesn't seem like it requires a lot." He turns my way, grabs my hand, and starts to walk away without giving the guy or the dog walker a second thought.

"No need to be such a fuckin' asshole, man! She said she was sorry!"

"Walker, wait … that wasn't nice. You shoul—"

"Keep walking, Blaire."

easy **virtue**.

I glance back and watch the stranger standing in the middle of the street with the biggest fucking grin on his face while the dogs play around him, forgotten. I drown out Walker's tirade as I grin back.

chapter six.

AFTER HE THROWS THE KEYS OF his Aston Martin to the doorman outside his building, Walker drags me to the elevator. As the doors close in front of us, he lets go of my arm and stands next to me without making eye contact. But the moment we walk into his place, Walker lifts me by the ass and carries me to his bed.

He unzips his pants, pulls them and his briefs down in one swift movement, his cock already hard. He doesn't bother to take my clothes off, placing me on his lap, and entering me in one hard thrust. With his hands on my bare ass, he drives my movements, propelling me to ride his cock mercilessly. Up and down. Tilting slightly back, my fingers grip his thighs as I watch his cock pulling in and out of me, the erotic visual drugging my senses. All I see is him penetrating me, his glistening cock entering me, and all I want is more. And harder. The slap of our skin fills my ears as he fills me. He's fucking me so hard it hurts, but it's a pain that borders on delicious pleasure, like all good things in life.

"Fuck … I'm going to come … I'm going … fuck …" he groans as I feel him tense underneath me with the power of his climax.

After he comes inside me, he pushes me off his lap, making the bed bounce as I land on it. Without looking at me, he stands up, his dick still hard and coated with his cum and my arousal, and makes his way to the bathroom.

I stare at his dark blue ceiling, trying to steady my heart and put my rambling thoughts and emotions in order. After a peculiar night filled with so many strange encounters, I'm drained. Yet I feel this sort of crazed energy pumping through my veins, keeping me awake. Walker's behavior after the accident outside the museum was nothing but odd. He didn't speak one word to me on the entire ride back to his apartment.

When I hear the toilet flush, I turn in the direction of the bathroom door and watch Walker shut the light off and make his way back to bed. I feel my cheeks flush as I watch him walk toward me in all his naked glory and it makes me want to fuck him again. The thought of him moving inside me as his fingertips grip my skin, crushing my bones with their ruthless power, fills me with a sick yearning for more. Always more.

"You never disappoint, Blaire. Did you see the way Arthur was staring at you? How fucking jealous he was of me?" He laughs, running a hand over his disheveled hair. "He wanted you so bad."

I stand up and take my dress off, throwing it on the floor, and cleaning myself up. Once that's taken care of, I get back in bed. Reaching for the white silk sheet twisted by my ankles, I pull it up to my chin, the fabric cooling my hot skin even though I'm cold on the inside. He gets under the sheets next to me, tangling our legs together. As I'm running my foot along his calves, feeling his smooth skin graze my toes, he pulls me close until my breasts touch his chest and my core grazes his soft cock.

"Is that why you started fingering me in front of your business colleagues while he watched?" I ask carelessly. The coldness inside me keeps spreading, numbing me more and more.

48

"That was something else. Only someone like you would let me do that in a room full of people." I can hear the smile in his voice.

"And what kind of person am I, Walker?"

"Oh, you know what I mean …"

"No, actually I don't. Could you please explain that to me?"

"You know, wild and gorgeous."

"You forgot the easy part. You forgot to add how easy I am," I answer, surprised at how cool and detached my voice sounds.

"Blaire, baby … you know that I love everything about you. Everything about you drives me insane. From your gorgeous brown eyes to the way you—"

I yawn, beginning to feel drowsy from a deep physical and mental exhaustion. "Walker, I'm too tired. We should turn the lights off. I need to go to sleep. I have work tomorrow."

"Take tomorrow off and spend it with me," Walker says before planting a peck on my lips. "I'm sure they won't miss you when they already have so many hostesses on staff."

"I can't. Lana's studying for finals, and I promised Carl I'd cover for her."

"Suit yourself." He gives my ass a tight squeeze, then rolls away from me to sleep on his side.

As I begin to fall asleep, the usual loneliness that has been my companion for as long as I can remember takes over me, and I welcome it. It's soothing and familiar. Every relationship I have is similar to this. Fuck, play, fuck, play, with no emotions attached to anything we do. But I'm okay with it. It's better that way because that means there's less of a chance of me ever getting hurt by anyone.

easy **virtue**.

My last thought before falling asleep is that I've been with Walker for months now and he doesn't even know the color of my eyes.

The next morning, we're in his expensive kitchen surrounded by black marble countertops and stainless steel appliances, the aroma of freshly brewed coffee floating around us. Walker stands in front of me, looking perfect as usual, wearing an expensive Tom Ford suit. I watch as he pulls out a white envelope from the inner pocket of his suit. "Before I forget … here you go. This should cover your rent for the next couple of months."

I take the envelope from his hands and open it, eyeballing the amount of bills inside. There's more than two months worth of rent in there. "This is too much." I frown, lifting my eyes to stare at him. "Are you planning on dumping me and that's why you're giving me all this money?" I tease.

Walker rubs his eyes with his palms.

Okay …

"About that, Blaire … " He sighs. "How can I say this without hurting your feelings?"

I take a step back, feeling the edge of the countertop behind me. "What is it? Just spit it out, Walker." A sick feeling settles in the pit of my stomach.

"My girlfriend is arriving from Paris tomorrow and I'm expected to propose to her in the next couple of weeks. So yes, I can't see you anymore."

I feel like I've been punched in the gut.

"Wait … what? You have a girlfriend?"

He lifts a hand to touch me, but I smack it away. "Fine, be that way, but I was hoping you'd take the day off so we could have more time to talk about this. And yes, I have a girlfriend. Her name is Emma. I thought you knew, Blaire. Anyway, what did you expect? Guys like me don't settle with girls like you."

"No, you just fuck us until you're bored."

"Oh, don't give me that righteous bullshit, Blaire. I pretty much paid to fuck you every single time we got together. The clothes you're wearing, your fancy apartment ..." He looks down at my feet, then back up, derision shining in his blue eyes. "The shoes you're wearing."

I don't know why I'm so shocked. It's almost Shakespearean, really.

The user got used.

"Yeah, you're right. My pussy for your money. But at least I never pretended to be anything else. But you, on the other hand, lacked the balls to be honest and up front with me. And you better hope that your *friends* don't rat you out to your fiancée because I won't take you back."

"They won't say anything if they know what's good for them."

"I pity your girlfriend because there's nothing worse than dating a coward and a liar."

He takes two steps until he's standing so close to me, our chests rise as one. Anger reflects in his eyes, my eyes, poison running in our blood streams. "You didn't have to. Don't you know we can always smell the gold diggers?" He wraps my hair in his hand, giving it a painful tug. "And I might've been honest if you were worth it." Then he lets go of me, the force of his release making me hit the countertop painfully.

"You know, I give you a couple months until you're back begging me for another chance because your perfect fiancée won't let you fuck her in the ass. We both know how much you like that. But I won't. I'll find someone else like you in no time. I always do."

I watch him flinch with the ugliness of my words.

His nose flares in anger. "You're nothing without me but trash, Blaire. Now get the fuck out."

I laugh. I want to say that I'm obviously too good for him, but the words get stuck in my throat.

They are all lies.

I've always known who I am. No point pretending I'm a good girl with great values because that would be a complete lie. I like money too much. I like the safety it offers. The power. And all the things I can buy with it. But as I turn around, walking out of his kitchen and leaving Walker behind, I realize I've done it again. I've made myself vulnerable, breaking my promise, a promise that I would never let someone hurt me.

And that's exactly what Walker has done.

I may not have physical scars. And in many ways my life has been easy compared to others who grew up on the streets or have faced cruelty at the hands of people who're supposed to protect them. But there's nothing like a bitter dosage of neglect and lack of attention from your parents while growing up to fuck with your head and sense of self-worth.

Trust me. I know.

As I get in the elevator with its cherry wood covered walls, smelling the fake clean cotton aroma embedded in the rug, feeling my heels sink in it, I wonder how I got here. I don't love Walker, but it still hurts. It hurts because someone else just proved how unworthy of love I am. So as I wait to make it back to the lobby, watching the numbers of floors decreasing, I recite that old and familiar chat.

Love is selfish.

Love is unkind.

Love hurts.

It wasn't his fault though … he didn't make me do anything. It was all me, and maybe that's why it's so painful. I have no one to blame but me.

I look down and try to slow down my breathing. I'm not a crier, so I can't say that I want to cry, but I am hurt. And my pain is clearing a path for anger to follow with regret one step behind.

When I step outside the building, the doormen avoid me as if they already know I'm an outcast and not welcomed anymore. I glance down at my body dressed in the same outfit from last night; I look like a hooker and *feel* like one. As humiliation and heartache fill every crevice of my body, I decide I need to move. I'm attracting too much attention standing on the corner while I wait for a cab. Maybe my feet will take me away. Maybe my feet will take away the pain that comes with the knowledge of who I am.

After a couple of minutes pass, I'm calmer and standing in front of an entrance to a subway station. Laughing, I have to be honest with myself. What did I expect? How can I be angry with Walker for using me when I was pretty much doing the same? It was his money, his name, and his handsome face that attracted me to him at first, so if I'm hurting at the moment, it's my fault because I let my guard down.

As I walk down the stairs, submerging myself in the subterranean darkness, the acrid smells of pee and sewage fill my nose. I scrunch up my nose at the subway perfume while I avoid stepping over a homeless man sitting on the bottom step. And because it looks like he could use a cup of coffee more than me, I take a twenty out of my clutch and hand it to him.

"Oh, thank you, miss! Thank you!" he says, smiling a toothless grin.

"No problem," I say as the kindness in his eyes makes my heart contract.

I'm about to close my clutch when I see my ticket out of this mess. My heart starts to beat faster as I grab the card and hold it in between my fingers. *Maybe that upgrade came sooner than I'd expected.*

chapter seven.

That night…

I STAND IN FRONT OF MY MIRROR once more and take in my appearance, applying lipstick over my bruised lips until they are a dark red. I observe how, layer-by-layer, I create my phony façade until I'm Blaire again. Until I hide all of my flaws.

But I'm a fraud.

As I continue to stare at my reflection, I remember a memory I had forgotten about. And it paralyzes me.

"Mommy! Mommy! Don't leave!" I cry desperately. My arms are wrapped tightly around her middle. My mom tries to push me away, but the harder she pushes, the harder I grip her. I can't let her go. "No, Mommy, please stay! Don't leave me. Please, please, pl-lease."

Tears stream down my face. The pain goes on and on, but I continue to beg her and hold her. I hope that she will hear me this time. I hope that she sees how much I need her.

"Blaire, let go," she says, struggling to break free from my hold. "I can't stand being in this house with your drunk of a father for one minute longer. It's driving me insane."

I hear wild laughter behind us. I turn to look at my daddy as he walks into their bedroom, making his way toward the edge of the bed where my mom's suitcase is lying open. His eyes are bloodshot, his untucked dress shirt has a greasy stain in the middle that spreads like spilled ink, and he's slightly swaying with every step that he takes. My heart contracts when the smell of alcohol surrounding him hits my nose. Grief laced with fear flows like a muddy river through me.

"Don't beg, Blaire. Only weak people beg. Let her go. She'll come back, like she always does," my dad says.

My mom turns to look at my dad, scorn in her eyes. "Don't fool yourself, Oscar. I'm not coming back."

"But what about me?" I cry.

My mom's gaze lands on me, softening a little, but then she turns to look at my dad and hardens instantly. "I'm sorry. I just can't do this anymore." She closes her suitcase and walks out the door.

"No, no, no, no!" I cry desperately, running after her, but she doesn't stop walking. She doesn't stop until she's out the door, leaving me behind ...

Sick to my stomach, I want to run toward the bathroom and throw up, but I fight the feeling like I fight everything else. I won't let Walker or memories of my parents win. Like the strong conquer the weak, I will conquer my emotions. *And really, it's not like Walker's desertion is the first one in my life.*

So I'm going to do what I do best. I'm going to erase Walker from my life. I'm going to pretend that he never happened or existed, burying any kind of feeling and emotion so deep within me that my heart and head will forget they exist in no time. And like the vicious cycle that my life has become, I'll find someone else.

I always do.

I have one goal in mind. To find out who Mr. Rothschild was.

I sit on my bed, open the computer, and Google his name. I skim the articles written about him in magazines and newspapers such as *Time*, *The New Yorker*, *NYT*, and *Forbes*. To say that he is rich would, honestly, be such an understatement. It becomes *very* obvious that he could, in fact, easily afford that necklace we saw and many more. He comes from old money from the Gold Coast of Long Island, and he is now the sole survivor and ruler of a media empire worth billions of dollars.

Once the truth settles in my mind that he is indeed as rich as King Midas and has a golden touch to boot, I decide to look at pictures of him. My eyes almost pop out of their sockets. There are images of him kissing more than a few of my favorite actresses on the mouth. He was married and divorced to a famous author, and was once engaged to a socialite with ties to European nobility. Apparently, at the age of thirty-eight, he has been married and divorced three times, plus countless numbers of flings. He has no kids. The word on the street is that he suffered a really bad breakup when he was young, from which he never fully recovered.

Hmm.

As I sit there, staring numbly at his picture on my screen, I can't believe my luck. Have I really met the goose that laid golden eggs?

The image of Walker's blue eyes and the poison reflected in them as he told me I was trash waltzes through my mind, but it already hurts less than it did a couple of hours ago. It already seems like a distant memory from my past.

Here's the thing: I erase people from my life.

The moment you become a liability, I discard you. If I get the sense that you will hurt me, I'll remove your existence from my mind and my heart, leaving a vacant place amongst so many holes within me. And I'm good at it. Once you're out of my life, I'll never think of you. I move on. You won't even have the pleasure of being an afterthought.

easy **virtue**.

You can call me heartless if you want, but the best way not to get hurt and not to get your heart broken, is by pretending that you lack one. And sometimes, I believe it. Almost.

So as I finish getting ready for work tonight, I erase Walker from my mind once and for all. It's better this way. And I decide to give Mr. Lawrence Rothschild a call since I have some time to spare before heading to the restaurant.

I reach for my discarded clutch on the floor, get his card, and grab my phone.

Sitting on my bed, nervously running my hands over my leather leggings, I wait for him to answer. After his phone rings four or five times, I'm about to hang up when he picks up.

"Hello," he says in that toe curling voice of his.

I grip the phone harder. "Hi ... um ... okay ... this is so odd, but we met last night at the Met. You gave me your business card."

"Ah ... did you grow tired of that boy you were with?" he says mockingly, sounding cool and detached.

"How do you—? You know what ... never mind. It's not important. I'm calling because I want to know what you meant exactly when you gave me your card."

"It means that I'm interested."

"Yes, but—"

"But nothing. I can tell that you're a smart girl. Why do you think a man my age would be interested in you?"

I grin, the nerves finally leaving my body. I know how to play this game. "I could ask you the same question, you know ... why would a girl my age be interested in a man of yours?"

He laughs in return. "Touché. It seems to me that we understand each other perfectly then."

I'm silent for a second, biting the inside of my lip. "Yes, I think we do."

"I'm flying to Hong Kong tomorrow morning for business but I should be back next Saturday. Meet me for drinks and dinner. We can discuss, for a lack of a better word, what exactly it is I'm interested in."

"Do you ever ask?"

"No. Why bother?"

It's my turn to laugh. I shake my head and say, "I'll think about it and give you a call ... or not."

"I get the feeling that you enjoy having the last word, don't you?"

"Blaire. My name is Blaire White. And, yes, but who doesn't?"

He chuckles. "Ah ... beauty *does* have a name after all. I'll be here when and if you're ready." He pauses for a moment, contemplating his next words. "And I hope that you will be, Blaire. I truly do."

With the ball back in my court, the last word is mine once again. "We'll see ..." I say before hanging up.

Unmoving, I sit on my bed as I wait for the beating of my heart to slow down, and wonder.

chapter eight.

"WHAT'S UP, GIRL?" ELLY ASKS when she sees me walking toward the bar. "You're early tonight."

Before I answer, I take a moment to watch Elly polish a glass with a white towel. Dressed in a skin-tight black dress, her short brown hair blown out straight, Elly takes my breath away. It's funny that the two of us are best friends. She's the kind of girl who doesn't need people's acceptance to feel good in her skin— to know her own worth. Whereas me ... well, let's just say that I need constant reminders.

"Um, you don't want to know." I sit on a black stool, spread my black leather covered legs in front of me and stare at my shoes to avoid meeting her eyes.

"Oh, Blaire ... who do you think you're talking to here? *Hello!* I'm your best friend and I can totally tell that you're lying to me."

I shrug my shoulders and continue to admire my shoes, tilting them in every possible angle. "Turns out you were right about Walker." I look up and smile. "Apparently, now that his girlfriend—soon to be *fiancée*—is coming back in town, I'm no longer needed."

Elly's eyes widen and her mouth drops open. "Wait, what? No fucking way."

Bored with my shoes, I lift my eyes and stare at my reflection in the mirror behind the bar. "Yep. What were his words? Let me think … Oh, got it! He said that guys like him don't settle down with girls like me, and then he proceeded to tell me that I'm just pretty trash and that without him I'm worth nothing."

Elly puts the glass she's cleaning down on the counter before she makes her way toward me. Once she's standing next to me, she wraps an arm around my shoulders as though she is trying to shelter me from pain. Her touch is comforting, but the gesture makes me twitch awkwardly in my seat. Men can fuck my mouth, bend me over a table, or do anything they want with my body. I don't find any of it as uncomfortable and unsettling as Elly's kind touch. I blame it on the years I went without my parents' affection. *Or maybe I'm just coldhearted.*

"Fuck him. It's his loss," Elly says.

I tilt my ass to the side, pull out my red lipstick from my back pocket and apply it. I watch as the bright color fills my mouth, enhancing the paleness of my skin and the blackness of my hair. "Whatever. He's officially part of the past. I've already moved on."

"But—"

"Listen, I guess if my life were a movie, this is where I'd stay home and cry my eyes out for weeks on end because I just had my heart broken by the man of my dreams. But that's not me, and that's not what happened, Elly." I turn to look at her, both of our gazes unwavering. "I dated him, yes, but it wasn't love. So I'm not going to sit around in my apartment sulking while I wait for him to change his mind and call me back. And I'm not going to wait for an apology because that ain't going to happen either."

"I get that, Blaire, but I don't think you're as indifferent as you—"

"It's fine, really. Anyway, does the name Lawrence Rothschild sound familiar to you?"

"I hate when you change the subject like that," she says, glaring at me.

I extend a hand, offering her my lipstick. "Does it?"

She shakes her head no, muttering, "Figures … another asshole. *Just* what you need."

I ignore her. Sometimes that's easier than facing the music or reality. *And reality can be such a cruel bitch.*

"We met last night at the exhibit. He gave me his card, which I'm glad I kept, by the way, since Walker ended up dumping me. I did some cyber stalking, and turns out he's a gold digger's dream come true. I gave him a call before I came to work." I omit the part about deals and possible money. I always have relationships with the men I suck dry because I don't do one-night stands. I'm not in it for the sex; I'm in it for the long-term benefits.

I get the feeling that whatever Lawrence offers will be completely different, and Elly won't like it one bit.

"Blaire, " she says carefully as if she's gauging her words and my reaction to them, "I don't want to be that nagging friend, but you *just* ended things with Walker."

"No, you're wrong. He ended things with me," I sneer.

"Whatever, and don't you take that tone with me, missy. Your bullshit won't fly with me. All I'm saying is that maybe you're hurting a little bit and that being with another guy is not going to make the pain go away. Don't let another guy use you or treat you like shit."

"Newsflash, honey, I use them too. Besides, I've had fun with most of the guys I've dated. I've been to Paris and Milan *just* for shopping sprees. I've fucked a guy senseless in the presidential cabin of the Oriental Express while touring Asia. I'm living in an apartment in Murray Hill for free, as long as I keep getting on my knees and opening my mouth. You call it being used, but I call it being smart and resourceful. All of my relationships are mutually beneficial. Trust me on that."

"But—"

I don't want to look at my reflection in the mirror anymore, so I get off the chair, feeling the slight thump of my heels when they connect with the floor. As I move to stand next to Elly, we stare at each other, resignation reflects in her eyes, *or maybe it's sadness.* The urge to cry comes over me, but as quickly as it comes, I'm able to control the slight trembling of my lips. I'm able to swallow over the knot in my throat and pretend that, for one short second, I wasn't tempted to get lost in the comfort of her warm embrace while I confessed that Walker had indeed hurt me; that I need my best friend now more than ever. However, the opportunity comes and goes, and like a departing train for which I'm too late, I watch the chance disappear over the horizon. I shake my head and lean down, kissing her cheek. "Can we drop it? I really don't want to talk about it anymore."

Elly shakes her head, making her short brown hair brush the outline of her jaw. "Fine, be your usual shit-don't-bother-Blaire self, but if you want to talk about it or if you need a good cry—"

"I'm not going to. I'm wearing my favorite Chanel mascara, and I like it too much to waste it on him."

She sighs. "Oh, girl, what am I going to do with you?"

"Nothing. Just love me like I love you." I smile and grip her hand, squeezing it hard. "Thank you, Elly. I mean it. You have no idea how much this means to me."

She squeezes my hand back. "Just know that I'm here for you, okay?"

I nod. "All right, get your cute ass behind the bar before I get you in trouble. I need to go talk to Carl about the computer at the hostess station. I think Carla messed up the program because some reservations won't show up," I say.

Later that night, when the restaurant is at its busiest, I smile at the couples waiting to be seated as I go over my conversation with Elly in my head. I don't want to explain to her why I called Lawrence because it would mean having to admit that Walker actually hurt me. That he managed to get under my skin when I least expected it and, like the Trojan horse, showed me how vulnerable I still am by cracking the indestructible walls I thought I erected. He showed me that they were breakable.

If I'm honest with myself, I feel like shit, but I will make sure that *never* happens again. I'm Blaire White after all.

I don't wallow.

I don't cry.

I move on.

I forget.

I discard … or get discarded.

I'm a survivor.

I'm resilient.

I will always have the last say in what goes on in my life. I've gone through too much not to. And if that means maybe getting involved with someone who is actually willing to pay me to sleep with him at the expense of feelings, so be it.

I don't care.

chapter nine.

I'M LYING IN BED TRYING TO figure out what to do with my day. I don't have anything going on until work later tonight, and staring at my white ceiling fan while I wonder if the blades could actually cut my head off is not what I consider healthy or fun.

I shake my head, dismissing the morbid thought, and stretch my body, yawning. Minutes pass in silence where the only sounds I can hear are my steady breathing and the noises coming from outside the window.

I grab my old copy of *Persuasion*—my favorite novel—and try to get lost in the love story of Captain Wentworth and his Anne Elliot. But today, not even Jane Austen's witty narrative will do. I'm restless and I can't focus.

Putting the book down on my nightstand table, I get out of bed and go to the bathroom to take a shower. I have to get moving so I can avoid thinking about what the hell I'm doing with my life and what is my purpose to exist other than sucking a rich man dry. It's quite annoying because as easy as it is to lie to everyone, it's close to impossible to lie to oneself since deep down we always know whether we are a failure or not.

And, oh, boy, don't I know it.

I decide to spend my time shopping. Yep, that's something that doesn't require much thinking, and there's no woe that a great outfit won't solve. And if it doesn't, at least I'll look good.

After I settle on a cute chocolate-brown, bohemian babydoll dress with a very delicate flower pattern, and loafer ankle boots, I take a shower and finish getting ready. But as I apply my makeup, I think that maybe I shouldn't go shopping since I need to make Walker's money last until I find someone else. I guess one of the reasons why I've managed to stay debt free for this long is because I only splurge when I'm dating someone who will take care of the bill. I try to avoid tapping into my personal savings account.

But then I remember Lawrence …

After buying a short leather skirt and a silk cream blouse with black piping, I leave Barneys. I'm standing outside the department store, watching people walk past me or cross the street, oblivious to the world beyond their minds, so I decide to take a walk as well.

I end up sitting on the wall at the Bethesda Fountain in Central Park. Once I place my shopping bag on the ground, I lean forward, dipping my fingers in the cool, greenish water as I look up at the famous Angel of the Waters. There are about a dozen pigeons scattered on its wings and hands, but only one sitting atop the statue's head. He looks lonely. My eyes remain trained on the bird until it flies away, then I scan the surrounding area protected in trees.

The heat is rising. The air is hot and humid, almost oppressive, and the light sheen of sweat that covers my skin makes the dress I'm wearing cling to my body. I'm staring at the young couple making out to my right, when someone sits next to me, his or her leg bumping into mine.

Out of reflex, I glance to my left and find a boy of maybe five or six years eating a salted pretzel. It looks delicious, and I guess my stomach agrees because it grumbles loudly in protest. Self-conscious, I wrap my arms around my middle as I realize that I haven't eaten anything all day. The boy must hear the embarrassing sound because he turns to look at me, smiling sweetly.

I flush. "Sorry about that."

"It's okay, my belly growls all the time. Mommy tells me that I eat like a champ because I'm growing up." He breaks off a piece of the doughy bread and hands it to me. "Would you like some? It's really yummy."

My mouth waters as I stare at the piece of bread in his hand, but I don't want to take it. I don't do carbs. At all. It's a hang-up I have, particularly because if I close my eyes and concentrate hard enough, I can still remember being cruelly teased about my weight by Paige and her friends.

I shake my head slightly. "Thank you, but no."

"Here. I promise I won't make you buy me another one."

The way the boy is staring at me, his hand holding the pretzel toward me, his soft brown eyes expectant, tugs at my heart. *How can I say no?*

I reach for the bread, smiling. "Okay, you win. Thank you."

"You're welcome." He grins from ear to ear before taking another bite.

I stare at the piece of bread in my hand. *Oh, what the hell.* After taking a bite, I address the little boy. "You were right. It's really yummy."

"Yep, told you. My name is Ollie by the way."

"Nice meeting you, Ollie. I'm Blaire."

He grins. "We can talk now since we know each other, doll."

I want to laugh but somehow I get the feeling that it would be crushing for the young boy, so I don't. "Doll, huh? Did someone teach you that word?"

"Yep, I got my skills from the best," he says proudly, but then his nose scrunches up. "He doesn't know I was listening to his conversation with his floozy. I was supposed to be focusing on doing my homework while they watched tv in the living room—"

Okay. I have to laugh. "Floozy? Where did you hear that word, Ollie? I hope he didn't call her that name."

"Oh, no! I heard my mom using it."

"Did she know that you were listening?"

He blushes and looks down at his feet. "No …"

Giggling, I realize that I haven't been this entertained in a very long time. Who knew innocence would be this sweet and fun?

I'm about to take a second bite when it dawns on me that he's alone. Frowning, I ask, "Hey, where are your—"

"Ollie! There you are, buddy! I told you to wait for me with Frank!"

I turn in the direction of the voice. The sound stirs my memory, and when my eyes land on the man addressing Ollie, I know why. Shocked into immobility, all I can do is stare at him, the same guy from outside the Met, as he takes me in as well. A stunned expression crosses his sun-kissed face that I'm pretty sure mirrors mine.

"Hi," I say, suddenly nervous. "Does this cute little guy belong to you?"

As soon as I ask, I see the resemblance. Glancing between them, I notice that they both have the same wavy coffee bean colored hair with natural golden highlights under the sun. Ollie's curls are long and untamed, but the man staring at me with the most unusual, striking light brown eyes, has short hair, the top longer than the sides. They both have the same straight and elegant nose, but the man's nose is dusted with freckles, giving him a boyish air. He's absolutely sigh-inducing.

He puts his hands in the back pockets of his jeans and smiles, making his eyes crinkle at the corners. "Maybe. Has Ollie been bothering you?" His voice is husky and deep, reminding me of old school Hollywood actors.

I look down at the grinning boy as he pushes himself closer to me. I smile and wink at him. "Not at all. As a matter of fact, he was kind enough to share his pretzel with me."

"Yep, I was a good boy and shared like you and mom always tell me," Ollie says.

"That's my boy," I hear the stranger say. The thought that he might be married is disappointing, which is totally ludicrous because I don't even know the guy.

After taking a few steps, he sits down next to Ollie. As he wraps an arm around Ollie's shoulders, his free hand ruffles his hair, making the kid giggle. "You scared the hell out of me, buddy. I went back to Frank's looking for you and you were gone. I need to text Frank and let him know that I found you before he loses his shit. Seriously, you can't do that again. I'm going to have to tell your mom and I'm pretty sure she's going to rip me a new one."

Ollie's shoulders fall contritely. "I know, Uncle Ronan. I'm sorry. I got bored listening to Frank talking to his girlfriend so I left. I just wanted to sit here."

Uncle Ronan? Hmm, I like.

The man, who is actually a lot more handsome than I remember, lifts his eyes, meeting mine, and smiles. "I can't say that I blame you, buddy. But you can't do that again. Promise?"

"I promise, Uncle Ronan."

I blush and lower my gaze to the ground but watch out of the corner of my eye as they shake hands. With his attention now on Ollie, I take the opportunity to check him out. The light caramel color of his skin lets me know that he spends a lot of time under the sun or outdoors. The sexy scruff on his square jaw says he hasn't shaved in a couple of days, and the muscles in his arms, strong like corded steel, show that he likes to work out. He reminds me of a model for Gap—laid-back, sexy, and oh so very cool with a dash of rock star. I don't think I have ever seen someone look as masculine and sexy as he does in a simple black fitted T-shirt without being totally douchey.

I continue to appraise him when his gaze connects with mine again and he smiles, almost as if he knows I've been watching him the entire time.

Figures. He just caught me staring.

I smile back because, really, what else can I do?

"Sorry, I'm being rude. I forgot to introduce myself," he says.

"No worries. You must be the one who taught Ollie all his killer skills with the ladies."

He runs his hand through his hair, groaning. "Do I even want to know?"

I shrug, enjoying myself immensely. "Oh, I don't know … doll."

"She seemed to like it too. She started making these funny noises and telling him not to stop and to keep going," Ollie adds proudly.

I grin when I hear Ronan curse under his breath. *Poor guy.*

Leaning forward, he places his forearms on his legs and turns to look at Ollie and me, his eyes dancing with mirth and a slight blush covering the crests of his cheeks. "Glad you two are having such a good time at my expense."

"Well … you asked, right, Ollie?"

Ollie nods his head vigorously, making his curls bounce. "Yep."

Ronan laughs out loud, pulling Ollie closer to him and mussing up his brown hair, making him giggle. It makes me smile too. "You little rascal. You're supposed to be on my team."

"She smells nicer than you, Uncle, and she's prettier too."

I grin. "See—smart boy."

"Jesus. How can I compete against that?"

"You can't," I say, laughter embedded in my voice. "I'm Blaire by the way."

"Blaire," he says, letting my name roll off his tongue. "It suits you. It's very pretty."

"Thanks."

"So, Blaire ... tell me, how is the dude in the tux?" he asks offhandedly, looking down at the ground as he runs his hand over his scruff. Though, by the way the muscles in his arms tense while he awaits my answer, I get the sense that he cares.

"You like to get straight to the point, huh? He's gone."

Ronan lifts his head to look me in the eye, all traces of laughter in his face replaced by something sincere, something tender. "Can't say that I'm sorry to hear that."

I want to speak, but the way he's watching me, almost as if he can truly *see* me, creates complete chaos within me, leaving me tongue-tied. His soft brown gaze wrecks every single thought of mine.

Our eyes remain locked as a sweet smile crosses his lips before he speaks once more, only further messing with my head. Really, I'm so busy watching the way his full and oh so kissable lips move that I've completely missed whatever he said. "I'm sorry, I didn't catch that," I say breathlessly. *Why the fuck am I breathless?*

He lets his eyes roam over my face, pausing on my lips. "I thought I would never see you again."

"Uncle Ronan ... I'm still hungry. Can I have a popsicle now?" Ollie interrupts. His words, like a hammer, break the thick brick of tension that surrounded us a moment ago. And I can't say that I'm sorry for it.

Sighing a breath of relief, I happen to glance at my watch, noticing the time. *Shit!* It's past four, and I still have to go home and get ready for work.

I stand and stretch my stiff legs after sitting for such a long time, noticing that the couple who was making out next to me are gone. Actually, the crowd is completely different from before, and the heat also feels less suffocating, less stifling. Funny how time seems to fly when you're having a good time. After I pick up my almost forgotten shopping bag off the ground, I turn to look at Ollie and Ronan as I tuck a flyaway strand of hair behind my ear.

"I'm really sorry but I have to go. I have an appointment in less than two hours, and I still need to catch a cab. It was great meeting you, Ollie and *Uncle Ronan.*" I wink at Ronan.

He smiles crookedly at me, shaking his head. "You have a thing for walking away from me, don't you?"

I bite my lip, as I recall that night. "And you have a thing for stalking, don't you?"

"Maybe I do ... maybe I don't. Maybe it's destiny playing its hand." He pauses, grinning cheekily at me. "Or maybe I just have a thing for nice scenery."

Laughing out loud, I whack his knee with my bag. "You're bad."

"Uncle Ronan ..."

I chuckle when he interrupts us once again. I almost get the feeling he's doing it on purpose.

"Yes, *Ollie?*" Ronan asks without breaking eye contact with me, amusement dancing in his eyes. That little boy is totally killing his game and he knows it, and if I may say so, quite successfully.

"Can I ask you a question?" Ollie asks.

"Sure."

I watch as Ollie pushes his little body closer to Ronan's and whispers something in his ear. Ronan shakes his head and smiles at me but addresses Ollie. "I don't know. Why don't you ask her?"

Ollie runs a hand through his long curls, making them look wilder than before. "I was wondering if you want to come to my birthday party tomorrow."

My heart skips a beat. I don't do birthday parties. I hate them. As panic begins to rise inside me, I have to cough a couple times to find my voice. "Oh, no-no-no ... ah ... I don't know ... I can't ... I'd be intruding on a family event. I just couldn't. Thanks for asking though, Ollie. That's really sweet of you."

Ollie shakes his head. "No! My mom won't mind, right, Uncle Ronan?"

Ronan pats Ollie on the back. "Nope, the more the merrier. Come on, don't break the boy's heart. It'll be fine." He turns to look at Ollie. "Right, buddy?"

"Yeah. Don't break my heart," he repeats meekly.

"You two are trouble, you know that, right?" I say as two pairs of brown eyes stare at me, waiting for my answer.

"But of the best kind. Don't you agree, Ollie?"

Ollie smiles, his baby dimples appearing. "Yep."

"I don't know, Ollie. We just met. I'm sure your mom is going to have something to say about inviting strangers from the park," I say, even though a part of me already knows that I'm going to go. I mean, how can I deny a child asking for me to celebrate with him when I know what it's like to want someone with you on your birthday but have no one?

"Oh, please, please, please come to my birthday party. There's going to be ice cream cake, hot dogs, hamburgers, and corn with lots of butter. And you can bring me a present. And we're not strangers! We shared a pretzel and you know my Uncle

Ronan. And I already like you better than my uncle's other floozy."

At this, Ronan's eyes look like they're going to pop out of their sockets. "Who taught you that word?" He groans angrily. "Never mind, I'm pretty sure that was your mom's doing. We'll have to talk about that later."

Not wanting to get Ollie in more trouble, I blurt out, "Okay, I'll come."

Ollie smiles smugly, his chastised expression from a moment ago evaporating into the air. "I knew you would, I knew you'd come!"

We exchange numbers and I type the details of his party in my phone (Ronan, the sneak, totally took advantage of the situation by saving mine in his cell). As I'm walking away, Ollie catches up to me, stands on his tiptoes, and whispers in my ear, "I think my uncle likes you, Ms. Blaire."

Tongue-tied and blushing, I turn to steal one last glance at Ronan and find that he's staring at me. When our eyes connect, the asshole has the audacity to wink at me before he breaks into one of those hypnotic smiles of his—and like an eclipse— I can't look away.

It's not until I'm in a cab on my way home that I realize I didn't remember to check out the brand of his watch. I don't think it would have mattered anyway.

chapter ten.

I'M NOT AWARE OF MUCH other than how nervous I am as I ride the subway to Brooklyn. Distracted, I got on the wrong train a couple of times which has made me terribly late. So now, on top of everything, I'm fidgety because I'm running behind. Fashionably late went out the window a train ride ago.

Why, oh why, did I let that little boy talk me into going to his birthday party?

I realize that a part of me wants to go and spend time with him and Ronan.

Ronan. Just thinking of his name makes me want to smile.

There are so many red flags in this scenario, but would it be horrible if I ignore them just once and have fun for a couple of hours? It's not like anything will happen between us.

I live in an apartment I can barely afford, I charged a major shopping spree on my credit card before Walker broke up with me, and my job is as a hostess. I have enough money in my savings account to last me for a while, but not if I'd like to keep up with my lifestyle.

Tapping my foot on the floor, I take my cell out and text Elly.

B: You're not going to believe where I'm going.

easy **virtue**.

Not a minute goes by before Elly texts back.

E: China?

B: Ha! Feels like it. I'm going to Brooklyn …
to a * kids * birthday party.

E: ?

B: Long story short. Met a cute kid at the
park. We shared a pretzel. Met his cuter uncle,
who I kind of know already. Got invited. Couldn't
say no.

E: Aww. Blaire does have a heart. <3 How cute
are we talking about here? PS I can't believe you
ate a pretzel. The guy must be really cute.

I smile.

B: The boy was very cute. But the uncle is
delicious. So much so that even my vagina wanted
to sigh. Imagine a Gap model with a dash of rock
star.

E: Shit. Not fair. Music is my higher power,
not yours.

B: Music makes your clothes fall off.

E: True story. Are you sure the uncle isn't the
real reason why you're stepping out of your
comfort zone and going to this *party*?

B: I can't deny that he's a bonus, sexy scruff
and all.

E: Ha. I knew it. You okay?

B: Not really. I'm freaking out. I changed my
outfit like ten times and ended up choosing the
safest and lamest summer dress I own. Do you

remember the white eyelet dress with the empire waist? Yeah. That one. Gag.

E: I love that dress! You look super cute in it. And you'll be okay, Blaire, just be yourself.

B: A self-serving bitch?

E: Nah. The self-serving bitch wouldn't be on her way to Brooklyn to a kid's party. Just be Blaire, the one you try so hard to hide.

B: To be continued … LOL.

E: You'll be fine! Okay, I gotta go. I'm having lunch with this very cute guitar player I met last night and I'm ignoring him for you. Love ya.

B: Lunch? Yeah right. Don't choke ;)

E: Pssh. Never. I swallow.

After I put my cell away in my brown leather satchel, I cross my legs as my bare skin glides over the plastic seat. Then I wrap myself in the protective cocoon of my arms, recline my head on the cool window glass, and stare ahead of me as we leave the city behind and head to Brooklyn. I watch as the view changes from subterranean blackness to a clear morning sky, buildings and cottony clouds replacing subway tiles and worn out posters. I tell myself to stop overanalyzing everything and just enjoy the day.

I'm standing outside a small house with a brick front and eggshell-colored shingles adorning the roof as I watch the gypsy cab that I'm pretty sure just ripped me off drive away. I shrug and turn to face the white wooden door as my eyes land on the gilded number four located under the peephole. I'm about to knock on the door when someone opens it. With my hand still hanging in mid-air, I watch as an older woman, maybe in her late sixties, smiles kindly at me.

"You must be Blaire. Ronan wasn't exaggerating when he described you to us. You're beautiful. I'm Allison, Ronan's grandmother and Ollie's great grandma. Anyway, come on in. The boys have been waiting for you."

"The boys?"

She glances back and smirks impishly, reminding me of Ronan. "Yes, *boys*. One more so than the other, though."

I blush, surmising the identity of both *boys*. "I'm so sorry for being this late. I got on the wrong train, only realizing it after it was moving and had to go back and change trains." I pause to take a calming breath. "I'm never this distracted. I—"

"Oh, dear, don't apologize. You know what they say … better late than never, right? Anyway, follow me. The party is in the backyard."

"Thank you," I say quietly, liking the silver-haired woman already, but even her kind eyes don't soothe my nerves. I feel like I'm going to be sick with every step I take that brings me closer to all the boisterous sounds and laughter—and to him.

We walk past a faded but comfortable looking green couch and love seat, a worn out dining room table with a centerpiece made out of fake looking wild flowers, and an even smaller kitchen with an outdated stove and fridge. As I take in my surroundings, I notice how different our lifestyles are. Not that there's anything wrong with what I see, but it isn't what I'm used to.

As soon as she opens the backdoor, the hot summer air blasts us in the face and everyone turns to look at us, growing silent.

With sweaty palms and a dry mouth, I raise my chin pretending that all the stares and silence don't bother me one bit, yet the pounding in my chest won't let me fool myself. I'm uncomfortable and nervous underneath my expensive armor. No Gucci heel has been known to slay a dragon, after all.

I'm about to ask Allison for Ollie's whereabouts, when I *feel* Ronan stand next to me before I see him. Without asking for my permission, he takes my hand possessively in his, like he owns it, and squeezes it once. He doesn't say a word, and I don't think it's necessary. His warm touch is all the support I need. I lift my eyes to meet his and watch him smile reassuringly. It's a sweet smile that softens his face, making him appear more beautiful than I remembered. A smile that makes me want to soar in the sky because no man has ever smiled at me like that.

"You came."

Dispassionately, I notice that my hands are trembling a little. It could be due to nerves, or maybe it's because Ronan's gaze licks every inch of me as it travels down my body—checking me out unabashedly. It doesn't matter. Whatever the reason is, it doesn't change the fact that Ronan has a way of crumbling my composure.

"Of course I did. I said I would, didn't I?"

Allison coughs, reminding us that we're not alone. "Ronan, show Blaire around and introduce her to the family. I'm going to go look for your sister and let Ollie know that she's arrived. Here, let me take that for you," she says, pointing at the plastic bag in my hand that holds Ollie's gift.

"I didn't know what to get him … there were so many toys and different collections, so I got him the entire set of Teenage Mutant Ninja Turtles. I remember watching that show as a kid and enjoying it, so I thought that he might too. Anyway, the gift receipt is there in case he wants to exchange it."

She pats my shoulder softly. "Don't worry, sweetie. He'll love it," she says to me before turning to look at Ronan and addressing him. "And you behave yourself, Ronan."

We watch as she makes her way down the wooden stairs of the porch toward a green plastic patio table filled with presents. The table next to it is covered in all sorts of food including macaroni salad, coleslaw, and potato salad. Out of the corner of my eye, I notice that people have resumed their conversations and aren't looking our way anymore. As relief courses down my body, I turn to look at Ronan, and his eyes are already on me, watching me closely.

"You babble when you're nervous, don't you?"

I groan and close my eyes in frustration. "Yeah, and I hate it."

"No, don't ... it's cute. Endearing, actually."

"You say that now. I'll ask you again at the end of the party."

Silence fills the space around us as we stare at each other, our smiles slowly fading.

"You look beautiful today," he says hoarsely.

"Thank you," I murmur.

He lifts a hand and touches the hot crest of my cheek, the contact electrifying. "Why are you blushing?" I laugh. Does he really need to ask? "Don't tell me you're not used to compliments because I won't believe it."

I lift a hand and cover his with mine but don't remove it. I'm not ready to lose the warmth of his touch. "No, it's not that. It's just the way you're staring at me. I can't explain it without sounding weird."

"Maybe I can explain it for you ..." The space between us becomes a magnetic field where the vivid intensity of his gaze draws me in, incapacitating me from all coherent thought and movement. "When I look at you, I see something I really want. Something I need."

All I can do is nod, releasing the breath that I didn't know I was holding up until now. Ronan's eyes crinkle at the corners, amusement making them sparkle. He totally knows he's gotten to me. "How's that for an explanation?"

"Good." I swallow hard, my heart beating faster. "*Very* good."

He grins cockily. "I'm glad you came, Blaire."

"Me too."

"Hey, Ronan! Stop drooling over the poor girl and help me get the grill going!" a man shouts.

Everyone laughs around us, which makes me blush even more. He winks at me before letting go of my hand. "All right, all right. Don't get your panties in a bunch! I'm coming. Everyone, meet Blaire, my future wife."

I'm smiling at everyone but as my mind registers his last words, I start coughing incessantly. What the hell? Patting me on the shoulder, I hear Ronan ask close to my ear, "Too soon?"

"Um, yeah? We haven't even kissed."

"Oh, is that an invitation?"

I smack him on the shoulder. "Of course not!"

"But you want me to?"

"No! I mean, yes. Grr … I don't know." I squeeze my eyes shut because I don't even know what I'm saying anymore.

He places a hand on the curve of my hip. His touch is tender yet possessive. "That's good enough for now. And just so you know, I'm not letting you walk away from me this time. No dogs, no assholes, no appointments. Today you're mine."

I don't want to smile because if I do I'll have to acknowledge how much I like the sound of that, but I end up doing it anyway. My body seems to be at odds with my brain—the slut. "Oh, really?"

81

"Ronan! We're starving here!" someone else shouts before he gets a chance to answer.

He leans down, gripping my hip softly, and whispers in my ear, "Nothing like being cockblocked by your own family, eh?"

As I watch him run down the same wooden stairs to finally join his family, I lift a hand to trace my lips and realize that I'm smiling. And this is when the butterflies kick in. Fuck.

I'm screwed.

chapter eleven.

"HERE, USE THIS," RONAN HANDS ME some paper towels to dry my skin. We were just about done with lunch when the skies opened, and it started to pour out of nowhere. Between all of us, we barely had time to bring the rest of the food inside before it got ruined with the rain.

"Thank you." I begin patting myself dry, conscious of the way Ronan is staring at me. It's been like this all day. Furtive glances here and there, smiles that seem to be for each other alone, innocent touches that burn brighter than the best of foreplays. The tension keeps rising, and the undeniable attraction grows sweeter with each second that passes by. Really, it's hard to concentrate when I look at him, imagining what his stubble would feel like in between my thighs … those full lips … how soft they seem …

God, this man is making me horny.

I shake my head and dismiss those irrelevant thoughts because they won't happen—I won't allow it.

I'm working on my neck, tilting it slightly to get under my chin, when Brian, Ronan's cousin and a charming flirt, comes up to me and wraps an arm around my shoulders.

"So, Blaire, how about you dump Ronan's sorry ass and let me show you what a good time is?"

"Oh, yeah?" I ask teasingly. The cute kid, who probably isn't older than eighteen, has been joking with me all day, making me laugh every time. Sadly, I don't think Ronan has found it as funny as I have.

"Yes, ma'am. The best kind."

"Brian, back off," Ronan retorts with a dangerous lilt in his voice.

"Oh, stop it you two," Jackie, Ronan's sister and Ollie's mom, says as she walks past them, smacking both on the back of their heads. Laughing, I watch the young woman with the exact same coloring as Ronan and her son turn in my direction and roll her eyes as she mutters, "Boys. Blaire, if you're over the *raging* testosterone in the room, you're more than welcome to come to the kitchen with me and hang out in there until it's time to bring the cake out."

I pause for a second, considering if I should. Up to this moment, it hasn't been too bad because Ronan has always made sure to stay close to me. Not necessarily next to me, but in the same group. His family has also gone out of their way to make me feel welcome, almost as if I'm already one of them. But this is completely different. This means that I'm going to have to talk to his sister without any kind of buffer, and I'm not sure I want to risk her not liking me.

When I first sat down to eat, I wasn't sure what to make of all the interactions. These people seem to genuinely like each other and appear to be a very tight-knit family, which is nothing like my own. Growing up, my house was always quiet and empty, especially during birthdays. There would be gifts but that was it. No laughter. No hugs. Nothing.

A handsome and relaxed Ronan owned the grill with a beer in hand as I shot the breeze with his grandfather and his pervy, yet sweet uncle who continually teased me. I watched Ollie and his cousins laugh and play with water guns.

And I was overcome with fear.

I didn't want to move, or speak, afraid to have all these lovely people dislike me—shun me—like so many had before. Because, for the first time since I could remember, I actually cared what they thought about me. I wanted them to like me as much as I liked them, even if I'd never see them again. For one short day, I wanted to know what it felt like to be part of a family like Ronan's, where love seemed to be the glue that held them together.

As I stare at the familiar color of her kind eyes, my gut tells me to go for it. "Sure."

After she asks me to sit, I watch her coat the vanilla cake in delicious fudge, her hands nimble and sure. She looks like she has done it many times before. "I've been meaning to thank you for what you did back at the park. Ronan told me that Ollie walked away from Frank and that he found him sitting with you. You have no idea how much I appreciate it."

"Oh, you don't have to thank me. I didn't do anything other than talk to Ollie. At first it didn't even cross my mind that he was alone but once it did, it seemed a bit strange. I was about to ask him if he was there with someone when Ronan found him. He seemed very worried."

"Yes, he'd better have been worried. Thank God Ollie didn't wander too far. I still get shivers just thinking about it. Anyway, I'm glad you came, Blaire. Both of my boys seem to be very happy that you're here."

Nervous, I pick up a spare napkin lying on the table and begin tracing the face of Thor. "I'm happy to be here." I take a deep breath, adding, "It's a great party. You have a charming family."

"Thank you. So tell me a little about yourself. Do you go to school, work?" she asks, her eyes briefly landing on my expensive shoes. "Nice shoes, by the way."

I cough, trying to clear my throat. "Thanks. Um ... no school, just work. I'm a hostess at Homme."

"I've heard of that restaurant. Fancy place."

"Yeah, it's okay."

She puts the spatula down, but not before she offers me some fudge. I shake my head no, but watch her helping herself to some. "Yum. This is some good stuff. You're missing out, Blaire. Anyway, I *do* have a charming family. I'm so lucky to have them. As you've probably guessed, I'm a single mother. When I was eighteen, I met this older guy, you know, in college and lived in the city." She smiles dryly. "I was swept away by the attention he gave me, the nice restaurants, the love confessions ... I thought I loved him. However, fast forward a couple of months later and I was pregnant and alone. I told him I was expecting and he dumped me, told me that it probably wasn't his child. I didn't know what to do. Our parents died in a car accident when we were little, so I couldn't talk to my mom. I ended up coming clean with Nana and Papa. Long story short, without their support and Ronan's, I don't know where Ollie and I would be now."

"I'm so sorry to hear that," I say, truly moved by her story.

She shrugs, making the blue strap of her dress slide down her shoulder. "Oh, don't be. I learned my lesson. But you must be wondering why I'm telling you this. Call it the mama bear in me, or maybe I'm just protective of my own, but, Blaire, and I mean this with no disrespect—"

"Whenever someone starts a sentence by saying that they mean no disrespect it's because they're about to insult you, don't you think? They're just apologizing beforehand. It's what I'd call a gloved slap to the face, maybe?"

She laughs. "I like you. You're ballsy."

"I'm just honest."

"Good, but back to what I was saying before. I like you. There's something about you that doesn't bother me like the other girls my brother dates." She raises her hand, stopping me from replying. "Not that you two are dating, I know, but I can already tell that my brother seems to be more into you than anyone else I've ever seen him with. He hasn't stopped smiling since you got here. I guess what I'm trying to say is that if you're just passing your time with my brother until the next guy with a Benz shows up, end it now before it starts. I know my baby brother. When he loves, he loves with everything that he has, everything that he is. Just look at him and the way he is with Ollie. My brother treats my son better than some fathers treat their own sons. It's not my place to say anything more, but that man has given up a lot for Ollie and me, and it's only fair that I watch out for him. Protect him. Even if it comes at the expense of sounding like a lunatic and scaring you before anything has happened."

I lower my gaze and notice the shredded remains of the napkin on my lap. *Did I do that?* "No ... you're just looking out for your brother, which I totally get."

"Right."

Lifting my gaze again, I stare her in the eye. "I don't know what you want me to say ..."

"Nothing. There's nothing to say, just lots to think about."

The most uncomfortable moment of the evening is when Ollie comes running toward me, grabs my hand, and guides me back to the table where everyone is gathered.

"Can I sit on your lap?"

I know what's coming as I watch Brian turning the lights out and the glow of candles coming from the kitchen. This is the hardest part for me and one of the major reasons why I avoid birthday parties. The cake combined with the fucking happy birthday song. A song that I can't sing without feeling a tight knot form in the back of my throat, without tears burning my eyes, without getting choked up during the first verse.

I want to say no to Ollie. I want to get up, turn around, and bolt out the door, never looking back. I want to run away from memories of a lonely girl on her sixth, seventh, eighth birthday—the list goes on—without a fucking cake because her parents forgot what day it was. Or, I want to run away from memories of kids making a point to exclude me, not inviting me to their parties and then talking about them in front of me.

But I do none of those things. I fight those painful memories like I fight everything else.

"Sure, Ollie," I say, noticing how calm I sound when everything inside me is in utter turmoil.

Ollie sits on my lap as the room goes dark and everyone gathers around us, ready to sing. I'm placing my hands on Ollie's shoulders when Ronan leans down close to my ear, his hot breath hitting my skin, "Don't move. I want to take a picture of you," he whispers, kissing me softly under my ear.

Before I have a chance to reply or react, my senses muddled with the ghost of his lips on my skin, I see the blinding flash of a camera. And then everything happens all at once. People around me start singing *that* song while Ollie grips my hand in his, his little body tense with excitement, or maybe it's my own body tense with dread. In a daze, I look up and watch everyone singing to him with smiles on their faces and love reflected in their eyes as the cake is placed in front of us. I glance between the candles dancing in the dark, to Ollie's earnest and pure smile, to those around us, and try to take everything in. A mundane scene for those used to it, but not for me.

As I sit there surrounded by so much, feeling so much, I'm afraid to move and wake myself up only to realize that I've been dreaming all along. I'm afraid that I'll open my eyes and everybody will be gone and that I'll still be that child who cries herself to sleep. But as a balmy sensation coats my body—my soul—I realize that this is real. That I'm not dreaming. But this moment isn't mine. This wonderful experience doesn't belong to me. It's borrowed, like everything else in my life.

I reject the thought as quickly as it comes. There's no room for reality. There's no room for starkly sad truths. I've given myself one day to enjoy without having to worry about what tomorrow will bring—without having to put on an act. So I join in the chorus, not caring that my eyes are blurry from tears, or that I can barely sing without choking. For once, there's happiness around me and I'm not alone.

After Ollie blows out the candles, Brian turns the lights back on, and my gaze lands immediately on Ronan as if I've known his location all along. The sounds slowly drown out in my ears, his family members forgotten as we stare at each other.

I smile.

He smiles.

And right now that's all that matters.

chapter twelve.

TENSION FILLS THE AIR, HIS BODY so close to mine I can feel the heat radiating from him, our legs rubbing together as we ride the train back to the city. With my hand safely encased in his, my head reclined on his shoulder and his delicious woodsy smell whirling around us, I'm happy. Content. I feel safe. I'm not even bothered by the fact that it's close to midnight and we're both alone in an empty car.

"Thank you so much for inviting me to Ollie's birthday party, Ronan. I can't tell you the last time I had such a good time. It was"—I pause to swallow, my throat suddenly constricted—"very special for me."

"Thank Ollie, it was all his doing. I had nothing to do with it."

I look up and raise an eyebrow skeptically, which makes him laugh in return. "Yeah, right. Keep telling yourself that if it makes you sleep better, buddy. But in all seriousness … it was a lovely party. The look on Ollie's face when he opened all his gifts was priceless, and probably my favorite part of the night. He looked so happy."

I tear my gaze away from him and stare ahead of me, watching the lights of the buildings illuminate the city's skyline. I don't know if it is the magic of the day or his intoxicating presence, but suddenly I find myself sharing painful memories that I thought I had forgotten long ago. "When I was about seven or eight years old, I was obsessed with this Hello Kitty watch I had once seen on a girl at the park. She was there with her parents, and she looked so happy. I remember seeing them play hide and seek and listening to their laughter drift in the air. Anyway, I guess in my young and really confused mind, I thought that if I had her watch, I'd have a little bit of what she had. Maybe, I'd be happy too. I begged my mom for it. Cried for it. I was only a child so you can imagine how melodramatic I was. My birthday came, Christmas passed, and she never got it for me. She thought Hello Kitty was childish and a distraction. I was crushed, so seeing Ollie's face when he got everything that he wanted and wished for meant a lot for me. It made me feel hopeful, you know? Like the world doesn't completely suck."

He tightens his grip around me, his touch comforting. I turn to face him. "Don't say anything. I didn't tell you that so you'd pity me. I just," I shrug, "I guess I'm still thinking about it. That's all. Anyway, you two are very close, right?"

Ronan stares at me for a moment, looking as though he wants to keep talking about me, but I guess he realizes I'm done with the topic because he follows my lead. "Yes, we are. He's my little man, always helping me with the ladies." His tone is playful, but the pride shining in his eyes tells a different story. I can tell that Ronan loves Ollie as if he were his own.

I bump his shoulder. "Jerk."

He kisses my forehead softly. "Hey, don't hate the player, hate the game. Besides, he got me a date with the prettiest lil' thing I've ever seen."

"You don't say?"

"Yep. She's got this sexy mouth, a body to drive a man wild. And when she looks at you with those damn near perfect blue eyes of hers, you kind of find yourself forgetting how to breathe."

"Oh my God, you have no shame." I shake my head but smile nonetheless.

He looks very pleased with himself as he grins smugly, his eyes crinkling at the corners. "Nope, at least not when it comes to you."

I know I'm blushing, but I can't help it. My body loves the compliment. *Traitor.* "Nice camera, by the way, Casanova," I point at the black case next to him while trying to ignore the heat shooting up my arm when his thumb lightly brushes my palm. "I noticed it back at the house."

"Thank you. When I'm not working my day job, I like to call myself a photographer."

Disappointment stirs in my chest as the reality of how different he is from what I typically look for in a man begins to dawn on me. I guess the day's magic is beginning to fade into reality.

"Wow, that's awesome."

"Yeah, it's mostly commercial stuff, like fashion spreads, book covers, and some high society stuff. It pays the bills and I enjoy it, but my dream is to see my work in a museum or art exhibit someday."

I lift my head from his shoulder and stare at him. When he mentions high society events, I want to add that I'm surprised that I haven't seen him around, but I keep my mouth shut. I don't want my other life to burst this beautiful bubble just yet. I want to keep him separate for as long as possible, even if it's only for the remaining minutes of the train ride. Because for now I get to pretend I'm a different Blaire, one with a different past—with different goals. "I'm sure it will happen."

He chuckles. "You haven't seen my work. How would you know?"

"Oh, I don't know, you seem to be a very talented man. The way you flipped those burgers in the air took my breath away. And let's not forget your skills with the ladies ... those are a killer," I tease.

"What can I say? I have many talents," he says, a devilish glint in his eyes.

"I'm sure you do," I say sarcastically.

He surprises me by grabbing my waist and pulling me closer to him. "And many of them can't be listed on my résumé," he whispers in my ear, his breath makes my skin prickle in awareness.

I laugh nervously, but when our gazes connect my smile freezes in place. His eyes, hungry and burning, make me uncomfortable because whatever I see in them, I want.

"Ronan, I don't think—"

"Shh ... I'm going to kiss you now or I'll lose my fucking mind."

He grabs the back of my neck and pulls me closer to his mouth, his touch sure and possessive. Before we kiss, as our breaths fuse, there is a moment where it feels as though everything goes still.

No sounds.

No movement.

No breathing.

No hearts beating as one.

Nothing.

It's a moment where the only thing that matters is to finally feel his lips on mine, to discover his taste. It's a moment when everything hangs in a fragile balance, waiting to be tipped to the other side. It's a moment full of what ifs, but I don't care as long as I get to taste him once, even if it's the one and only time.

As the intensity of his eyes sear through me, and the forceful touch of his fingers pulls me closer, I decide that it doesn't matter. *As long as he becomes mine for the seconds of that one pulsing kiss.* When our lips finally touch and our tongues fiercely meet, the contact tilts my world upside down, annihilating me. I know that there is no going back. At least not for me.

With one kiss, Ronan has managed to break me.

By the time we pull apart, I barely open my eyes and gather my wits before he wraps his hands in my hair and brings our mouths close once more.

"I think we can do better than that," he murmurs huskily against my lips.

"We can?" I ask breathlessly. *Is it even possible?*

"Definitely."

"But—"

"Blaire?" He tightens his hold.

"Yeah?"

"Shut up and kiss me."

This kiss is different. It's as unapologetic as it is rough and needy. It's carnal bliss. It makes my head swirl. It makes me tremble. It makes me feel him from the top of my head to the tips of my toes and everywhere in between.

Once the kiss ends, we slowly move apart until we're staring at each other. We breathe heavily, the space between us a magnetic field where the force of his eyes draw me in, making it impossible for me to look away.

"Fuck," he exhales deeply. "Now *that's* what I call a kiss."

"Wow," I manage to say, feeling as though a firecracker has gone off inside me.

He stares at me for a moment too long, his thumb softly rubbing my tender lower lip. "I want to kiss you again ... so fucking bad."

I smile as I look around the train car, making sure that we're still alone. I stand up and straddle his lap. As our bodies touch intimately, I feel a blush as hot as hellfire burn my cheeks and spread through the rest of my body, centering in my core. I'm a human bonfire of lust burning brightly for him. His eyes on me, he covers my bare thighs with the palms of his hands. At first I think he's going to go deeper between my thighs, but he surprises me. He pulls the skirt of my dress down, making sure that my body isn't exposed to the public eye in this position. My heart melts a little with his protective and cavalier gesture.

Grateful and horny, I wrap my arms around his neck and pull myself closer to him—our bodies rubbing—until the front of my knees touch the plastic seat. This close, and with only a scrap of cotton protecting me, I can feel the contour of his very hard cock nudging me, driving me wild.

I smile, feeling bold. "About that kiss … what are you waiting for?"

I watch the cocky, one-sided smirk that frames his lips turn into a full-blown electric smile. "Jesus Christ. With my fucking pleasure, beautiful."

And he does. He kisses me until nothing exists beyond him, beyond this moment. We become two swaying bodies in a tempest of desire and yearning, with no end in sight. Ronan kisses me until I forget my name, forget who I am, forget that this isn't supposed to happen, and, most importantly …

Forget that it can't.

Ronan stands outside my apartment, ready to say good-bye. One hand rests possessively on my hip as the other caresses my swollen lower lip. I can feel his thumb lightly grazing over a cut from one of his many kisses.

"I think we got carried away." He smiles lazily.

I smile back, feeling my hot skin tingle from his touch and a ride full of memories. "Maybe we did."

He leans down and places a soft kiss on my nose.

"What was that about?" I ask.

Ronan smirks, running his hand through his hair and disheveling it a little. "Just felt like kissing your nose."

"Weirdo," I tease.

We stare at each other in silence as all traces of a smile slowly disappear from his handsome face. Then he steps closer to me until his front touches mine and places his hands on the door, enclosing my head. "I want to see you again, Blaire," he whispers against my mouth. "Go out with me tomorrow night."

I shake my head no. "Ronan ... don't. Please, I can't go there. Today was probably one of the best days I've ever had. The party ... the train ride ... it was all ..." I take a deep breath and exhale slowly. "I shouldn't have kissed you, but I couldn't help myself. But we can still let the night end on a high note. Don't ask me for another date, or to see me again. I'm not good for you. I'm really not."

He frowns. "Why don't you let me be the judge of that?"

I want to stamp my foot in frustration because he's making things so difficult for me. He isn't supposed to fight back. He's supposed to accept my answer without asking any questions. He's supposed to leave.

"I just got out of a relationship, Ronan. I'm not ready to date." Lawrence's green eyes flash in my head. After taking a deep breath, I push all thoughts of Lawrence into the dark recesses of my mind and focus on Ronan. I can't let him seduce my thoughts with his memory and what it promises.

Ronan smiles and lifts his hands to cup my jaw tenderly. "Blaire, I'm not asking you to date me. I'm just asking for another chance to see you again."

"I don't know—"

"Don't be scared of me."

"I'm not scared of you. I'm scared of myself, and of the things you make me want, and—"

He shuts me up with a kiss that I feel all the way in my bones. When he pulls away, he's totally rocking a smug expression on his face. The asshole knows the power of those lips of his, and knows exactly how to use them to his advantage. "Fuck me … it just keeps getting better and better."

"Huh? What? What keeps getting better?" I ask, fluttering my eyelashes open.

Ronan lowers his face and begins trailing kisses on my neck. Every time his lips come into contact with my skin, little shockwaves spread through my body, over and over again. "Kissing you, Blaire. It keeps getting better and better."

I swallow hard, my legs turning to jelly. "You really need to stop doing that."

"What? This?" he whispers roughly before kissing me once again.

"Oh …" I sigh into his mouth before I realize that he's done it again. I smack him on his solid chest. "And you did it again! You better stop it, Ronan, honestly. I can't think when you do that."

He grins. "Good, I don't want you to. Go out with me, Blaire."

I shake my head, fighting a smile. "I know I'm going to regret this."

"Maybe … but live a little."

"I like my life to be planned and uncomplicated."

"It's better to live a life full of regrets than not live at all." He lowers his voice and adds huskily, "Let me show you how it's done."

easy **virtue**.

"What makes you think you have what it takes?"

After he roams my face hungrily with eyes that burn with passion, he leans down to whisper in my ear, his breath tickling my skin, "I've got what it takes. Trust me on that."

"This is crazy, but fine. You win."

He smirks like the sexy man that he is, charm oozing out of his every single pore. "Aren't the best things in life the ones that make us feel a little crazy? A little reckless?"

I bite my lip and let his words sink in, wondering if he's right. "I don't know about that ..."

"I guess we'll just have to find out, won't we?" He moves away from me, my body already missing his warmth. Eyes on me, he starts to walk backward toward the elevator. "And in the meantime, stay away from the streets."

"Why?"

"Because you're a heart attack on legs, beautiful."

I laugh and cover my face with my hands as I stare at him through the gaps between my splayed fingers. "Oh my God. That was so bad."

Ronan smiles a sweet smile that emphasizes how beautiful he is, but that isn't what makes my heart leap. It's the way he's staring at me. What I see in his eyes. "It made you laugh, didn't it?"

"Yes, but—"

"But nothing. I wanted to hear you laugh."

I roll my eyes and laugh, the sound free and light as I let the moment sink in.

Ronan ... it could be so easy to fall in love with you.

chapter thirteen.

I TAKE A DEEP BREATH, FLIP ONTO my stomach, the fluffy pillow underneath my cheek soft and comforting, and stare ahead. The shadows of the night disappear as rays of sunlight bathe the room in a golden glow. Ronan dropped me off sometime after midnight, but I haven't been able to fall asleep. When I try to close my eyes, my mind replays my entire day with Ronan over and over again, sending my heart into overdrive. My body still hums with energy and giddy excitement, forcing sleep away.

I watch the morning breeze coming through the open window, making the white curtains dance lightly against the windowpane. The movement is fluid and free—so peaceful to watch, so different from the storm brewing inside me. Not even the frenzied fluttering in my stomach, or the slow burn between my thighs as I remember his touch, can keep my thoughts at bay. The angry voices shout inside my head that he's bad for me and that I should tread carefully, but I try to quiet them for as long as possible. I just want to pretend for a little longer that I'm normal; that someone actually likes me for who I am, and maybe that someone could grow to care for me.

My heart rate accelerates as I recall what it felt like to kiss him. What it felt to have his arms wrapped around me like he was never going to let go. What it felt whenever he smiled at me and only me. I try to distinguish the feelings coursing through me in the Ronan aftermath.

Is it happiness?

Awe?

Satisfaction?

Hope?

Desire?

Fear?

I think it might be a little bit of everything. How can I describe the exact feelings that reign my body after what could possibly be the best day and night of my life? I'm giddy. I'm confused. I'm scared. But I'm so damn happy. For a day, I lived to the fullest.

Ronan showed me that there's a difference between living and *living*. And it wasn't that we were reckless or that we did anything outrageous … no. It's odd, but I *felt* every second tick by. Every laugh was real, every word we spoke meant something, every touch of his etched itself on me, and every kiss we shared embedded itself in my soul. There were no wasted or trivial moments.

Every single minute counted.

Every single second breathed new life into me.

I take a deep breath and try to control my nerves when I hear my cell ring. Call it sixth sense, but I immediately know it's him. As excitement runs through me, I get off the bed, my feet hitting the carpeted floor almost at running speed, and reach for my phone sitting on top of my dresser.

Motionless, I watch his name light up the screen and a smile so big it hurts my cheeks spreads across my face. I feel something akin to joy and delight running through my veins. My heart hammers inside my chest. About to reach for the phone, a thought crosses my mind.

I like him.

I really, really like him.

The phone keeps ringing and I keep staring at his name on the screen. Hesitation holds me hostage. Fear of the unknown cripples me. It's also fear that allows his phone call to go to voicemail, forbidding me to pick up. But there's a spark inside me, one that shines brighter with every second that passes by, its light breaking through the darkness in my heart.

Would it be so unforgivable if I stole a few more forbidden and happy moments with Ronan before he realizes how unworthy of anything remotely close to love I am? I've tasted heaven in Ronan's arms and I don't want to leave just yet.

Is it selfish of me? Maybe.

Is it reckless of me? Definitely.

But Ronan makes me want to let my hair down and dance naked in the rain. He makes me want to put Taylor Swift on and sing at the top of my lungs about how everything has changed because of a man with freckles and what I see in his eyes. And as long as I don't let my guard down, as long as I keep my eyes open and my heart tightly shut, I should be okay. I should be able to get lost in Ronan and his beauty for a little while without getting hurt.

Dear paralyzing doubts,
You can kiss my Chanel-clad ass (at least for now) and go to hell.
Love, Blaire.

I grab my phone and call him back.

"Hi," I say breathlessly.

"Hi, beautiful," he says, and I get the feeling that he's smiling.

"Sorry about missing your call. I—"

easy **virtue**.

"It's okay. You called back."

Yes, I called back ... I called back!

And just like that I know that I've never stood a chance against this man.

chapter fourteen.

Ronan.

Official Date #1:

WE MAKE OUT IN THE MOVIE THEATER like teenagers 'til our lips are sore and puffy. Note to self: Must watch the movie again when I'm not with him. Couldn't even tell you what it was about, other than it had people in it.

Date #2:

He takes me to his favorite restaurant in China Town and attempts to teach me how to use chopsticks. It's a complete failure, but he gets extra points for not laughing at me in my misery. *Like, how the hell are you supposed to grab peanuts with those things without losing them halfway to your mouth?*

Date #3:

He pulls me into his arms in the middle of a busy street, and there's a moment before his mouth lands on mine in which we stare at each other silently. No words are needed. No grand gesture. It's just him and me. A woman and a man finally finding each other in a world full of noise and distractions.

It's our beginning.

Date #4:

We dance close together in an almost deserted Central Park under the moonlight while he alternates between humming a Jeff Buckley song in my ear and kissing my neck, leaving me breathless.

Dates #5, 6, 7 …

It doesn't matter what we do as long as I'm with him. His face is all I see and his touch all I need. Being with him is simple. It's magic. He's summertime and his kisses warm sunlight. He makes me think of popsicles and laughter. He makes me feel free.

Whenever we're together, I can hear the fast beating of my heart, *feel* the blood rushing to my head, his nearness setting my body ablaze. Fear, delight, and thrill spin inside me, tangling with one another until I don't know where one begins and the other ends. But there's no time to think, or unravel my emotions.

I know I'm living some kind of borrowed dream and that when I wake up, I'll crash and burn, but I won't let reality intrude just yet. I can't.

So I finish getting ready to spend another stolen moment with Ronan. I run my fingers through the curls in my hair as I watch my reflection in the mirror above my bathroom sink. The girl staring back at me is a stranger. Her blue eyes shine brightly with a light that wasn't there before, and fire colors her cheeks. She looks happy … hopeful. A part of me wants to call her a fool, but I quiet that voice before it has a chance to make me see reason and ruin everything.

I close my eyes and let go of those thoughts with the shake of my head when I hear the doorbell ring. I take one last look at myself in the mirror, making sure that my cut-off denim shorts look good with my flowy Chanel white tee. Satisfied with my appearance, I fluff my hair one last time, smile, and make my way to open the door for him.

With his hands in the back pockets of his jeans, his brown hair perfectly messy, he looks scrumptious in a white linen shirt with its sleeves rolled all the way to the elbows. "Hel—"

Before Ronan even gets a chance to finish his sentence, I grab him by the forearm and pull him urgently toward me. Our chests flush against each other, I kiss him hungrily. Suddenly afraid, a necessity to make sure that he's real and that he's here, standing in front of me, takes over, and only his lips, his smell, and the feel of his body so close to mine will dissuade such need.

When we pull apart, our breathing is heavy, desire an invisible thread connecting us. In an unspoken agreement, we both take our time, savoring each other and not rushing things. But with each heated kiss and caress that we exchange, we test the limits of our sanity further and further, until control is almost nonexistent.

"Someone is happy to see me," he says huskily, a slow smile appearing on his achingly beautiful face.

I stand on my tiptoes, wrap my arms around his neck, and rub my left cheek on his chest. "You have *no* idea. I'm in so much trouble it's not even funny." And I am. I'm in so much trouble because this man is making me doubt myself and my goals.

"Here, Blaire." He places a finger under my chin and pushes it up until I get lost in his eyes. Lifting his hands, he buries them in my hair and pulls my face closer to his, our lips almost touching. Ronan traces the crests of my burning cheeks with his thumbs. "Babe, listen to me and listen carefully. If you're in trouble, I'm fucked. I was a goner the moment you smiled at me. I don't think I've ever wanted someone as much as I want you."

Lost in his eyes, eyes that own me, I can feel my pulse shoot up to the stars. "You're going to make me drown, you know?"

"I know … but I'm right there with you."

I giggle. "We're really fucked, huh?"

"Utterly fucked."

I smile. He smiles. And the world disappears.

Oh, Ronan, how you make my heart glow.

Before we head out, I go to my bedroom to get my leather bag. As I'm about to grab it, I happen to look at my dresser where my perfume bottles are, and something I've forgotten all about since I met Ronan catches my eye. Lawrence. His business card beckons me like the light at the end of a dark tunnel. I pick it up and trace its sharp edges as vestiges of our last conversation flood my memory.

"I'll be here when and if you're ready. And I hope that you will be, Blaire. I truly do."

I don't know what I'm doing with Ronan or what will happen between us, but the last thing I need right now is a reminder of my other life. *My real life.* So I push thoughts of Lawrence and what we talked about to the back of my mind.

I'm just having fun. What are a few more days?

As I paste on my first fake smile for Ronan, I ignore the little voice inside my head saying that time is almost up.

chapter fifteen.

"CAN I OPEN MY EYES?"

"Nope, not yet ... just a few more steps," Ronan says, opening what I think is a sliding door. I hear the city sounds play in my ear as the balmy air of an early evening in the summer whispers on my skin.

I extend my hands in front of me. "Fine, be that way."

Ronan laughs in my ear. "It's a surprise, you impatient lil' thing. I hope you're hungry though."

"I'm starving, but not for food," I tease, a playful smile on my lips as I reach behind me for the front of his pants.

"Good." He laughs. "We're here. I'm going to let go, but don't open your eyes until I tell you to."

"You know you're making it incredibly hard for me not to cheat, right?"

Ronan chuckles, his hands circling my waist. "All right. You can open them."

And when I do, my breath catches in my throat.

We're standing in what I assume is someone's private terrace at the top of a building facing Central Park. The sun is setting, casting amber and red lights across the park and the buildings surrounding it. It's as though the city is burning to the ground, the sky filled with clouds like cotton candy in all its shades of pink, purple, and blue. In awe, I turn to look at Ronan, who's watching me with a sheepish smile on his lips, the golden speckles in his brown eyes shining like winter lights.

"You mentioned the other day that you love sunsets."

Suddenly, I feel like crying. I don't think anyone has ever done something this special for me, let alone paid attention to what I've said outside of the bedroom. To most guys, I'm only a body they enjoy fucking and showing off. I don't think anyone has ever cared enough. That is ... until now.

I tuck some hair behind my ear with trembling hands as I finish admiring what Ronan has done for me. On the floor, there's a checkered picnic blanket and a wicker basket filled with cheeses, fruit, and wine. Not caring about anything but Ronan and the overflow of feelings pouring out of me for this man, I turn to face him.

He's watching me with his arms crossed, looking like he just discovered the cure for a deadly disease. Without sparing a second thought, I wrap my arms around his neck and my legs around his waist, and kiss him, open-mouthed. I kiss him with everything that I have and everything that I am. I kiss him with the passion of a woman tasting the promise of true love for the very first time in her life. Every man before him forgotten.

I break the kiss and stare at him, trying to find the right words to thank him, but all I can do is drink him in. Ronan pushes my hair out of the way gently. "Do you like?"

I nod. "I like. A lot." And because I don't know how to show gratitude with anything but the use of my body, I whisper against his mouth, "Do you want me?"

He leans down, his nose tracing my collarbone. "Indecently."

I lick my lips. "Take me to your apartment."

"Are you sure?"

"As sure as I'll ever be."

Ronan is quiet, but the way he's looking at me feels as if he is tattooing himself within me, within my soul. "Let's get out of here then."

The ride back to the Lower East Side, where his apartment is located, is quiet. We both realize what's about to happen and really, what is there to say?

We haven't kissed since we left his friend's penthouse; we've only held hands. The tension between us is heady and makes me want to throw up. I feel excited, nervous, giddy, jumpy, but I'm not scared. In a way, this feels more like my first time than it ever felt with Mr. Callahan.

Inside his room, I walk toward the bed and stop when I'm standing in front of it. I take a deep breath as I stare at his navy blue duvet before I turn around. Slowly, as an unsmiling Ronan devours me with his eyes, I take off my T-shirt and let it fall to the floor. Ronan reclines his back against the door, rubbing the back of his neck as he continues to watch me undress for him, naked admiration and want reflected in his gaze.

I take my shoes off next, curling my toes as I fight an epic battle with nerves. I want to laugh at myself. Here I am, what I would consider a worldly, promiscuous girl, feeling gauche for the first time in my life because of a man and the innocent emotions he awakens in me.

I unbutton my shorts and take them off until I'm left wearing nothing but a light-pink thong and bra. Many men have seen me undress and used my body until I couldn't walk, but right now I feel like the innocent virgin I never was. Not even

Walker came close to affecting me the way Ronan does. As a matter of fact, being with Ronan demonstrates how little I cared for Walker. How insignificant he was.

I'm about to unhook my bra when Ronan steps forward, placing his hands on my shoulders. "Not like this, Blaire." He runs a finger along the edge of my bra, the side of his finger tracing the curve of my breasts. "You have no idea how many nights I've lain awake imagining this moment … what it would feel like to have you in my arms. I want your mouth on me, your hands on me. I want to taste you … savor you … devour you until you're begging me to stop. I want to feel myself buried inside of you, moving in you, robbing me of all logical thought. I want to feel you tremble, hear you gasp and moan as I pull you tighter against me. I'll go deeper and deeper until both of us burn with desire and passion. I want to mark you. I want to fuck every other guy out of your body until I'm all you feel, all you remember." He leans down and nips my lower lip. "Tonight I'm not going to make love to you, Blaire. I'm going to own you. Do you hear me?"

I brush his cheek with the back of my hand, the contact scalding. "You already do," I say softly, and it's true. No one matters anymore besides Ronan.

No one.

Ronan lowers me to the bed and lies down next to me. Leaning over me, half of his body covering mine, Ronan lowers his head until his hot breath touches my skin, raising goose bumps all over. I close my eyes, trying to calm my rapid breathing when I feel his tongue gently tracing the beauty mark above my belly button. "You taste so fucking sweet," he says huskily.

I open my eyes to find him staring at me. His mouth begins to move upward, leaving a trail of soft kisses behind it. Slowly.

Decadently. The moment his lips land in the valley between my breasts, he pauses, smiling against my skin, testing my control. But fuck control. He isn't supposed to stop now. Groaning, I grab his head and pull him closer to me.

He chuckles before he mouths my breast, sucking it in. I tighten my hands into fists while I try to control the light trembling of my limbs, but I can't. Hot and cold chills scatter throughout my body as he continues to torture me. His eyes on me, I observe the pink tip of his tongue tracing the outline of my erect nipple, flicking it, turning the wet material a dark pink. "So damn sweet."

I moan and reach for my bra. He places a hand on top of mine, a devilish light in his eyes. "Not yet. I'm still having fun."

"Seriously?" I say breathlessly, my heart pounding.

He smirks. "Yeah. I told you, I'm going to take my time with you."

"You're impossible."

"You're beautiful." He lets go of me and stands up.

I turn on my side and watch him undress, feeling like I was just cockblocked. "Do you *ever* not say the right things?"

"I don't know." He looks at me, his gaze penetrating and full of something I understand but don't want to acknowledge. "Maybe it's because you make me feel all the right things, Blaire."

As he unbuttons his shirt, I observe his exposed muscles, showcasing a tattoo of a crouching tiger on his left pectoral. He kicks his Converse sneakers off with his socks, his jeans going next. Ronan stands in front of me wearing boxer briefs that mold to his thighs and ass, the perfect V between his hip bones and a raging erection sticking out like a bulls eye. *God, he's breathtaking.* When he turns around to close the curtains, I see an Asian-inspired black and gray dragon covering most of his back.

easy **virtue**.

I'm not sure what's more stunning—the artwork or him. It's probably Ronan who makes the tattoo that beautiful. Every thick groove and muscle on his back moves as he extends his arm. His body is art.

With the only light in the room from the lamp on the night table, he gets in bed behind me. "I need you closer than this," he says, wrapping me in a tight embrace.

With my back touching the front of his chest, he begins to gently stroke my thighs, the apex between my legs, lightly tracing my mound, my stomach. His touch is reverent, possessive. He pulls down the cups of my bra and lets my breasts spill out into his large hands. He cups them, his fingers lightly grazing my nipples, awakening them to his touch, awakening my body as it hums with the promise of what's to come. With each stroke, each caress, the man is engraving himself on my skin. He's learning my body as I learn his touch, and there's no going back for me.

I want to turn around, but he holds both my wrists in one of his hands, stopping me from moving, while the other begins to caress my ass, palming the soft skin.

"Don't move." His hand goes inside my thong, seeking my core from behind. He runs his tongue along the edges of my ear and whispers, "I want you like this. At my mercy."

He spreads my legs open with his free hand, hooking one behind his hips as one, two, three of his fingers begin to pump into me, stretching my opening. I tremble as I break free from his hold and place my hand on top of his. I follow the movements of his hand as he continues to thrust his fingers in and out of me, each time a little deeper, feeling how wet they become with my essence.

It's pleasure.

It's pain.

It's euphoria.

He pulls out and rubs my clit, making me feel as though life sprouted from his touch. "This," he breathes against my neck, "belongs to me now."

I laugh shakily when he pulls his hand out of my underwear, turning my head in his direction. I watch him raise his fingers to his mouth and suck them clean. Once he drags them out, the tip of his tongue traces the flavor of my body lingering on his lips. He grins, his eyes wolfish. "So fucking sweet."

"Ronan …"

"Shhh …"

"But—"

He kisses me, and I can taste myself on him. Is there such a thing as a pulsating kiss? A kiss that breathes life into you, a kiss you feel from the top of your head to the tip of your toes, a kiss that awakens your senses and makes them sing? Because this feels like it.

Ronan breaks away and begins trailing kisses from the valley of my chest to my belly button, down between my legs. Opening his mouth, his probing tongue traces the outline of my core through the wet lace. He breathes me in, inhaling my smell deeply into his lungs as though it was the last bout of air he'd take in his life. And then he nudges my panties aside, his fingers spreading me open until I feel the warmth of his tongue caressing my clit, licking me, plunging deep inside of me. I moan as he arouses every sensation in my body with his wicked mouth. Slow, fast, faster, slower, each swipe drives me closer to paradise. I want to die of bliss yet my body hums with life. He curls his fingertips up against my walls, never ceasing his divine assault. "You like this, Blaire? My fingers inside you, fucking you senseless?"

"Please, Ronan …"

"What do you want? Tell me. I want to hear you say it."

I watch him drive his fingers deeper inside me as he flicks my clit with the tip of his tongue. "I want you. I need you. God …" I pant. "Now."

He stops his torment and slides my thong off my legs. His tongue runs up my inner thighs, the back of my knees, each naked area the fabric touches as it leaves my body. He stands up, removing his briefs, puts a condom on his rock hard erection, and lies back down. Ronan then moves behind me, spooning me, and brings his cock to my entrance. But instead of pushing all the way in, he drags the pulsing head along my wet opening, grazing my clit.

"Mmm … you feel so damn good, Blaire."

The roots of my hair are soaked in sweat, my body in flames. I begin to grind my hips in circles, seeking his fullness, wanting him to fill me—own me. And he continues to tease me by pushing lightly into me, just to pull out. My eyes are closed. My breathing accelerates with each lustful second that passes between us. I'm so close to begging when he lets go of his hardness, grabs my hips from behind and pushes all the way in. Putting a hand in the middle of my back, he pushes my body forward and starts to pump into me. Our bodies tuned, we become one. At first his thrusts are shallow, his thickness impaling me, filling me, but like a slow train gaining speed, he begins to drive into me harder.

I push my ass toward him. "Deeper, Ronan. I need to feel you deeper inside me … harder."

He curses, placing his hands around my waist. Restraint gone, our hips slam violently, driving us closer to the edge. The room is filled with the sounds of wet skin slapping against each other. Flesh against flesh. So fucking fierce. So fucking beautiful. His groans. My moans. I begin rubbing my clit furiously as he fucks me from behind like a savage. His cock sinks deep inside me over and over again, the intensity of his plunges erasing all logic. He's everywhere, saturating my senses. And I give him my all. Skin against skin, we live through our bodies with every kiss, every glance, and every touch until we can't go on any longer.

"Oh, God …"

"Yeah, baby?" he teases, his voice strained.

I half laugh, half moan. He feels so good moving inside me, like sweet agony and painful pleasure all at once.

I'm so close. So close.

And then there's nothing but pure ecstasy surrounding me as I come undone. Ronan slams one last time inside me as a cry tears from his chest with the power of his climax. We're both left trembling and breathless.

I don't think I've ever felt more complete than at this moment with his throbbing cock still buried inside me and his hands bruising my skin with their demanding hold.

We bask in the after-sex glow, Ronan's arms wrapped around me. I trace the outline of the tiger tattooed on his left pectoral. A French quote runs along the back of the animal.

"What does this mean?"

"'What is essential is invisible to the eye.' It's a quote from *The Little Prince*. It was my mom's favorite book."

"Oh, I love that. I haven't read that book yet. I should check it out."

"You definitely should."

"So I guess this is the part where we're supposed to bond by sharing earth-shattering truths about ourselves."

"Yeah?" He tightens his hold on me and nuzzles my neck. "I thought we *bonded* all right."

I flick him on his side, making him chuckle. "Not *that* type of bonding, you pervert. I'll start. I love the smell of wet grass and old books. I'm a die-hard Janeite and I love dogs." I chuckle, remembering Jalina. "When I was a little girl, my mom found a mutt puppy abandoned in a cardboard box in the empty lot behind our house. She was going to take it to a shelter, but my dad told her to give the puppy to me instead. Anyway, I named her Jalina. My nanny told me that I would dress her in my mom's clothes and put makeup on her, and the poor dog wouldn't even bat an eyelash. God, I loved her so much. She was my best friend."

He kisses my bare shoulder before he grabs a strand of black hair and twirls it in his fingers. "What happened to Jalina, and what's a Janeite?"

"Old age," I say, feeling the familiar pang in my chest whenever I think of her. It's been nine years since she passed away and not a day goes by when I don't miss her. "And a Janeite is basically someone who's obsessed with anything about and related to Jane Austen. Okay, your turn."

"Let's see ... the details are muddled because it's been so long, but one of my favorite memories is of my mom holding her camera and taking pictures of my father while he painted Jackie's bedroom a light pink. I remember thinking she was the most beautiful woman I had ever seen. I think that's when my love for photography was born."

"How old were you when your ..." I hesitate.

He finishes the question for me. "When my parents passed away? I was seven. They dropped me off at school because it was snowing and they didn't want me to take the bus since the roads were covered in ice. They never made it back."

My heart breaks for the little boy that he was. "I'm so sorry, Ronan."

"It's okay, it's been a very long time. I just hate the fact that I have to look at their pictures to remember their faces. It's not fair, you know? They were so full of life, so fucking beautiful, and now all that's left of them are frozen and lifeless images on paper. By staring at those pictures, you would never know that my mom had the sweetest laugh and always smelled like cookies. And you would never know that my father loved to take Mom and Jackie in his arms and twirl them around the living room. Anyway," he smiles, a trace of sadness lingering in his gaze, "I have one more. Ready?" He tugs the strand of my hair wrapped around his finger, pulling me closer to him, and biting my lower lip.

I nod, lost in his eyes, in him.

"I met a girl and I'm crazy about her."

"Crazy, huh?" Fighting a smile from escaping, I lean over and rest my cheek on his chest as the beat of his heart fills my ears with music. "I hope she's nice."

He squeezes my ass with his hand. "She's all right. Can't keep her hands off of me though. But what can I say? Chicks dig me."

I push my body slightly away from his and smack him on his flat stomach. "Asshole. Chicks dig—"

Ronan laughs before silencing me with a kiss. When we pull apart, the air charged with electricity, we stare at each other without saying a word. We let the comfortable silence fill the space between his walls as we soak up the sensation of being in the arms of one another. Nothing has ever felt this right before.

"For what it's worth, I think your parents would be very proud of the man you've become, Ronan, and I mean it," I say hoarsely. "And now you can stop looking at me like that."

"Why?"

He looks so handsome with his lips all swollen because of my kisses and his hair all wild because of my hands.

"Why what?"

Letting go of me, Ronan rests the side of his body on his elbow and cradles his cheek in the palm of his hand. With his free one, he caresses the side of my face tenderly. "Why do you want me to stop?"

"Because." I feel myself blushing and I hate it. "You're looking at me funny."

And he is. His eyes are … I can't explain it. It makes my stomach flutter. It makes me yearn for things that I don't want, things I don't have the luxury to feel.

"And how is that?"

I'm quiet for a moment.

"I can't really say … I don't know."

He smiles, and there's so much tenderness behind it that it shatters me. "You don't know or you can't say?"

"Oh my God … just stop!"

I hide my face in the pillow and groan. When I hear him laugh at my reaction, I turn to look at him, murder written in my eyes. How dare he? "Are you laughing at me?"

Humor leaves his face, a serious, thoughtful expression now in its place. "I'm looking at you because, right now, that's all I want to do."

And that, ladies and gents, is what I call a knockout.

If I were a cartoon, I'd be lying on the floor with hearts and cupids twirling around my head. But there's a voice inside my head warning me that this thing between Ronan and me is becoming very dangerous. For the first time in my life, I've found someone who makes me *feel*—someone who could easily make me fall madly in love with him.

I know I should be afraid of what he makes me feel, of how much he makes me want to change, to be a better person, even try to become whatever he needs me to be. I should be afraid because he makes me want to let go of my fears, my hang-ups. He makes me want to give my whole self to him just as he has given himself to me. I hunger for the feeling I get when I'm with him because it almost fools me into believing I am the Blaire that he wants.

"What's the matter, babe?" Ronan must see the fear reflected in my eyes.

"Nothing … I'm just happy. *You* make me very happy," I lie, kissing him under the chin.

He's about to speak, but I stop him, placing my fingers on his mouth. "Shhh … don't say another word." I push myself closer to him, grab his hardness in my hand and stroke it, feeling the veins of his cock throb in my palm. "Fuck me, Ronan. I need you again."

"Your wish is my command."

I laugh. "How obliging of you."

"It's the gentlemanly thing to do, after all," the ass says, a devilish grin on his face as he reaches for a foil package.

Ronan kneels in front of me, pumping his dick in his hand as I spread my legs open and let him watch me begin to touch myself. I push my fingers shallowly into me and coat them with my desire for him and what's to come.

"Christ. You're beautiful."

He leans over me, his mouth finding mine. Placing one hand on the bedframe for support, the other seeks my swollen warmth, pulsing with fire for him …

Just a few more dates.

Just a few more days of paradise.

And then this will all be over. I have to end it.

There won't be any real harm done as long as I don't let him get any closer to me than he already has. He'll forget about me and move on. As they all have. Like they always do.

I just …

I just wish the thought didn't make me feel sick to my stomach.

chapter sixteen

WORKING IN AN EXTREMELY HIP eatery in Midtown means that
we get a huge influx of powerful men around lunch and
dinnertime. Politicians, executives, lawyers, and businessmen all
come here to conduct business (more like trying to assert who
has the bigger cock when they aren't stroking each other's egos)
while eating an overpriced piece of meat. It's one of the reasons
why I loved my job so much. This place is what you'd call the
perfect hunting grounds for someone like me. It's how I met
Walker ... and a few others.

And today, for the first time in a very long time, I wish I
weren't here. That thrill that I used to get when men looked my
way? Gone. That nervous energy that always had me on the
move and never satisfied? Finito. There's no noise filling my
head and disrupting my peace of mind. I'm a floating cloud on a
blue morning sky. I'm a loose leaf twirling in the air, dancing
with the breeze as my partner. I feel carefree. And Ronan has
done that to me.

I smile at a couple as I tell them that their table is ready, but
the smile isn't for them; it's for Ronan and Ronan alone. My
body might be here, but my mind is with him back at his small
apartment, making love on a warm bed. I might be standing here

dressed in Prada from head to toe, but I'd prefer to be wearing nothing but the scent of Ronan on me. Ronan is my new favorite brand.

"Blaire? Hello! Are you there?" Elly says, bringing me out of my reverie.

"Oh hey, Elly. How long have you been standing there?"

"Long enough to see that your mind is somewhere else, or with *someone* else."

I sigh, smoothing the nonexistent wrinkles away from my black pencil skirt. "Sorry. Yeah, I was thinking of Ronan."

She looks at me as though I had two heads.

"Brooklyn boy?" I remind her.

Elly smiles as she grabs my pen and twirls it in between her fingers. "I *knew* it. You've been acting funny this past month. And if you're telling me his name, things must be getting serious."

"They aren't. We're just having fun, and what do you mean *funny*?"

She shrugs. "You really can't see it, huh? And I don't know, you're always smiling now. And by the way you're glowing, I can definitely tell that you, my friend, got laid last night."

I roll my eyes but can't help smiling. "You're wrong. Well, partially wrong." I glance at her sideways. "I got laid last night *and* this morning."

"You loose woman," she teases.

I blow her a kiss playfully. "And proud to be one."

We laugh quietly, making sure we don't draw too much attention to us. "Elly, I don't know what I'm going to do. I really, really, really like him. It's scary how happy he makes me." I look down at my nails, noticing that my usually pristine manicure is chipping away. "But I'm not good enough for him. He's everything that I'm not. He's the kind of guy a nice girl should date, not one as fucked up as me."

"There're a few risks worth taking in this life," she says, grabbing my hand. "And love? Love is one of them, even if you don't know how it will end. Quit your ice queen act, drop your resting bitch face, and let things happen. You might be surprised at how they turn out. And, FYI, *everyone* is fucked up. Some people are just better at hiding it than others."

We stop mid-conversation when we hear the glass doors open and close. I turn toward the entrance, a ready smile on my face for the next customer.

But I freeze.

Because standing in front of me is Lawrence Rothschild looking as sinfully handsome as I remembered him. He's with a large party of suits, but my eyes only see him, drink him in, savor him, all men fading to a meaningless background next to him. As we stare at each other, I feel my body coming alive with desire—with an attraction that would be foolish to deny.

I clear my throat, pulling myself together. "Welcome to Homme," I say, my voice trembling slightly.

He smiles an easy smile, one that charms and unarms me at the same time. One that lets me know he's aware of how unsettling his presence is to me. One that pushes Ronan out of my head. "Hello Blaire."

My name on his lips is a soft caress and as inebriating as a kiss.

He's smoke; dark, dark smoke that clouds my senses, whispers against my skin, and fills up my lungs, polluting me with his intoxicating beauty. I'm about to answer him when I hear Elly politely excuse herself, saying that she has to get back to work. As she's passing by me, she whispers in my ear, "Don't sabotage yourself."

Focusing on Lawrence and his party, I nod without looking at her. Her warning angers me. She tells me not to sabotage myself, but what she doesn't realize is that my feelings for Ronan already have.

I'm changing.

It started with little things such as my clothes and my hair, even my makeup—less plastic, less suggestive, natural and soft. And today, it's work. I usually go over the schedule as soon as I get to the restaurant, especially if I'm not at work the day before when the confirmation calls go out. I like having an idea of who will be dining with us and how busy we'll be. I'm annoyed at myself because I've been too preoccupied with a man, letting my emotions mess with my head and my priorities, and not doing my job properly. Because if my priorities were straight, if I had my act together, I would have known that Lawrence, or as his name appears on the computer, Mr. Rothschild, had a reservation this afternoon.

Ronan and his sweet kisses have managed to turn my world upside down in a matter of weeks, making me feel as though I'm losing control over my own life. I'm breaking my number one rule which is to never think with my heart, and that's going to get me hurt. The heart is stupid. The heart is easily fooled, leaving you exposed and weak. And I'm angry with myself for allowing it to happen in the first place.

My manager, Carl, must have recognized Lawrence because before I have time to utter a word, he's standing next to me, welcoming him. He tells him that his table is ready and that it would be his pleasure to take him to it.

Lawrence doesn't even bother looking at him, his eyes holding mine captive, devouring me. "Actually, I'd like to have a word with Ms. White first." He pauses, the hint of a smile promising everything that is forbidden and wonderful on his lips. "Privately."

We're in Carl's office.

I'm standing in front of the metal desk and Lawrence is by the door, an entire room between us, yet I swear I can feel him as though he is next to me and our bodies are touching. We stare at each other in silence, tension making the small hairs on the back of my neck stand on end.

With his hands in his front pockets, his stance is relaxed and imposing all at once, but he doesn't fool me. He wants to intimidate me. He wants me to be the first one to break. However, I know how to play his game. I cross my arms and continue to stare at him in silence.

He's the first one to speak.

"I misjudged you. I thought that you would call, and I'm never wrong." He tilts his head to the side, his sardonic smile making the corners of his eyes crinkle with laugh lines. "I must say it's a novel thing, and one that I don't enjoy."

"Well, there's a first time for everything. But if you must know, I met someone."

He raises an eyebrow, probably thinking about Walker, and I have the decency to blush. "Someone else."

He chuckles. "And let me guess, this someone else, he's special?"

Suddenly I can't meet his eyes, so I focus on his burgundy tie, admiring the pattern. "Yes, he's very special. He's different ... he's perfect."

"Don't be so naïve, Blaire. He's human, therefore, flawed." Lawrence closes the space between us in a few ground-eating strides. When he's standing not even an inch away from me, I look up quickly and get lost in his green gaze. The color reminds me of an Amazonian jungle—so rich, so bright, endless.

The attraction undeniable, I watch him lift his large hands, cupping my face gently but with resolve. When his cool skin comes into contact with mine, I shudder as he crumbles my defenses with his tempting touch. He caresses my cheek, noticing the slight trembling of my body. "Would you like me to stop?"

As I look into his eyes, I know that I can't lie to him. "No."

"What is it about you that won't let me get you out of my mind? Is it your beauty?" Lawrence asks as the pad of his finger traces the arch of my eyebrow, the caress gentle as the summer breeze. "Your smell?" He lowers his face, tracing my jawline with the tip of his nose ever so slowly, ever so decadently. His soft, warm breath kisses my skin and makes me shudder. "The feel of you?" He brushes my hair out of the way with the back of his fingers. They leave a burning trail behind as he kisses the nape of my neck. "Or is it the way you taste?"

I'm enveloped in a hazy cloud of lust for a man I don't know. My chest rises and falls faster and faster as I gasp for air, his closeness making me feel as though I cannot breathe. The room spins. The temperature rises. I have to clench my hands tightly to stop myself from reaching out and touching him, the need to feel him under my palms overwhelming. The magnetism—the pull between us—growing stronger with each second that passes by, and I'm powerless to stop it. He's gravity and I'm the falling apple doomed to hit the ground. But Lawrence's hold on me goes beyond the physical. Lawrence and his luring words speak to the dark Blaire, to the Blaire I *have* to be, making it impossible for me to ignore him and his advances. That Blaire wants him. That Blaire can't say no to him.

Releasing a shaky breath, I say, "I've thought about you."

"Even with this special someone in your life?"

I lick my lips. His attention arrested, his gaze follows the tip of my tongue as it slides across my mouth.

"Yes. And I hate myself for it."

Silently, he traces my lower lip, wetting the pad of his thumb with the moisture that my tongue has left behind. I watch him raise his finger to his mouth, sucking it—tasting me. My core pulsates with hunger for those lips, for that mouth. The images of myself riding his face flash through my mind like blinking neon lights.

"My darling, you want me as much as I want you. Don't fight it."

I close my eyes momentarily as I'm hit in the chest by a rock heavy with guilt and self-disgust.

Ronan.

"Why are you doing this to me? I'm trying so hard to do the right thing for once."

"Because this"—he buries his hands in my hair and pulls me toward him, bridging the space between our faces—"is inevitable." Then he kisses me fiercely, and I swear I can feel the ground beneath my feet shake. His mouth, his lips, his tongue taste like sin but feel like heaven, making me forget momentarily that there's a man with laughing eyes waiting for me back at his apartment.

As we pull apart, he says, "Leave work. Come with me. My place is nearby."

"I can't."

"You can't, or you don't want to?"

I want to say that I don't want to, but the words get stuck in my throat. "You know the answer … but I can't. I've met someone who I really, really like. He's very special."

"And yet you're here alone with me, repeating over and over how special he is. I wonder, is it because you're trying to convince yourself of that fact?"

I place my hands on his chest, but I don't push him away. "I'm leaving. I'm not even sure why I'm still here."

"I'll tell you why," he says roughly. He lowers his hand between my legs, pushing through the fabric. I grab his shoulders for support and close my eyes as I feel him probing … imprinting me on his palm … on the length of his fingers. A desire so intense, I can't think, I can't move, shatters me to pieces. *Ronan is far, far away.*

"You feel this?" Lawrence says, thrusting deeper against the material. "Your pussy is so warm, I know you're soaking wet for me." Letting go of me, he raises the same hand that was rubbing me not a moment ago to his nose and takes a deep breath, smelling me on his fingers. "Your body, your scent, they betray you, Blaire."

And, he's right. I want him. A baser part of me, where lust, greed, and desire rule my mind, wants Lawrence and all of his millions. That same part of me wants him to fuck me until he eradicates Ronan and all the happiness he's brought into my life from my mind.

"Now look at me in the eye and tell me that you don't want me."

I stare at him, our eyes locked in a war with no winner in sight. "I may be a lot of things, but I'm not a liar."

Pleased, he smiles. "When you get bored playing house with your *special someone*, give me a call."

"I won't," I say, but even the words sound empty to my ears.

"Oh, but you will, Blaire. And you know it."

And then he turns, heads to the door, opening it, and walks out without once looking back.

chapter seventeen.

As soon as I'm done with work, I go straight to Ronan's apartment. I don't bother saying goodbye to Elly or calling Ronan to let him know that I'm on my way to his place. The less I think, the better it is.

All I know is that I must see Ronan.

All I know is that Lawrence is still in my head, playing games with me—screwing with my peace of mind.

Damn him.

I knock on Ronan's door harder than necessary, my knuckles stinging. When he opens the door, I walk in without waiting for him to invite me. The urgency to be with him grows stronger with each minute that passes. If I'm with him, if I feel his hands on me, if I hear his voice, and if I look into his eyes, he'll make the other Blaire—the one who wants Lawrence and everything he offers—disappear. He'll make her grow quiet once again, her wants and pragmatism forgotten.

He shuts the door behind me. "Blaire? I thought you were—"

Without saying a word, I close the space between us until our bodies connect. The outline of his dick touches my stomach, my breasts push against his hard chest, and the tips of my nipples tingle with desire. A primal urgency to have him, to take him, pulsates like the beating of my heart inside me.

"Ronan," I breathe against his lips. "Shut up and kiss me."

I grab him by the back of his neck, pulling him toward me, and kiss him. Our tongues clash in an open-mouthed battle, but it's not enough. Craving more of him, yearning for more of him, I deepen the kiss until he's everywhere. As liquid fire spreads through my bloodstream, I guide my hand past the waistline of his jeans and inside his boxer briefs, wrapping my fingers around his cock and pumping it.

He curses and begins to undress me, swiftly getting rid of my skirt and my panties. When he's about to remove my shirt, I pull my hand out of his jeans. "Not here, your bedroom."

His chest quickly rises and falls, his breathing heavy. "Woman, you're going to be the death of me."

I walk toward his room as I remove the rest of my clothes. I glance back, looking at him, and freeze. Even though I can see desire in his eyes, it's the tenderness behind it that makes me want to break down and weep.

Don't think. Don't think. Don't think.

When we're in his room, surrounded by warmth, books, and photographs of his travels, I push him toward the bed. "You stay here."

I move to his wooden chair by his desk where his camera and proofs are. I bite my lower lip, heat gathering in my core and a tingling sensation spreading through my pussy as I sense his eyes on me.

I sit on the chair, which happens to be across from him, my bare ass and back gliding across the smooth surface. Ronan watches me closely, his gaze, sparking with lust, roving over my figure. It reminds me of the way Lawrence looked at me back in Carl's office.

I watch Ronan get undressed. His black vintage Beatles tee goes first, his jeans next, and last but not least, his briefs. His cock, so hard, points toward his stomach. Ronan sits on the bed with his back against the headboard and his hardness in his hand, leisurely stroking himself.

A blatant smile on my lips, I spread my legs open and place them over the wooden arms. I'm completely exposed in this position as I cup my breasts, playing with them. The desire I see in his eyes is reassurance enough. It looks like he wants to do very bad, naughty things to me, and I am a more than willing victim. I want to be corrupted. I want to forget what happened with Lawrence. But no matter how hard I try, I can't. My body still vibrates with the memory of his touch, his kiss, how it felt when his fingers touched me there.

"Watch me," I say, trying to push memories of a green-eyed man out of my head.

Slowly, provocatively, I lower my hand to my pussy, spread my swollen lips apart, and rub my clit with the pad of my index finger. The slight pressure. The back and forth. The sweet humming of my senses as they come alive with my touch. *God, I'm wet.*

"Mmm, this feels good," I taunt as I begin to fuck myself, spreading my legs wider for him to see my fingers disappear inside me. My head lolls back, the sensation of them moving in and out of me, impaling me, heady and powerful.

I rub myself.

I grind on my hand.

I feel filthy, but I love it.

The sound of our breathing, the feel of my fingers inside me, my wet pussy contracting around them, the smell of arousal in the room and knowing that Ronan is seeing me masturbate inebriates my senses.

I'm drunk with lust … with him.

Ronan begins to thrust harder into his hand. A smug, half smile on his lips, he watches me watch him pump his cock up and down in his fist, the pace increasing, his hold tightening. My mouth waters, the throbbing and swollen head inviting me to suck it.

"Would you like a taste?" I pull my soaked fingers out and suck them clean, tasting myself on them. "Mmm…" I moan. "So good."

Ronan, the bastard, shakes his head as a smug smirk graces his face. "No, I'm good."

And then, because I'm not one to deny myself of bodily pleasures, I decide I've had enough. I'm feverish with want and nothing but his beautiful cock will do.

I stand up, my legs stiff and fire burning through me, and walk back to bed. When I'm standing next to him, I put my nose below his ear and breathe in his aroma of man mixed with arousal. Noticing the way his muscles tense by my nearness makes me smile.

"Really?" I whisper, licking his ear.

With my back facing him, I crawl into bed on all fours. In this position, I'm primed for him to take me from behind, and that's what I want. I want him to claim me in the most animalistic way. I want him to fuck the guilt out of me, and mark me as his own over and over again.

I glance back and wink at him saucily. Yes, it's an invitation, or a dare, and one I hope he accepts. With one hand, I spread my ass cheeks, burying my middle finger in my opening, and show him exactly where I want him, where I need him.

Ronan doesn't disappoint.

Our gazes connect, promises of the pleasure to come shining in them. Ronan kneels right behind me as he grabs a silver package from the nightstand, rips it open, and rolls it over his hardness.

He slaps my ass once, twice, making it sting just so he can soothe the pain with his tongue a second later. I watch him wet his right thumb with his mouth and lower it between the curves of my ass as he begins to glide the head of his cock against my entrance. He spreads open the folds of my pussy with it, coating himself in my desire, the tip caressing my clit. A purr escapes my mouth when I feel the rough skin of his thumb play with my forbidden place, teasing me, rubbing me to hell and back.

"Please," I beg.

He shakes his head, not even bothering to hide his smile anymore. "Not yet."

At that, I laugh out loud but it sounds more like a sob, my body shaking with need. *He's making me pay for my chair stunt.*

"Ronan." I pause when his thumb disappears inside me. I bite my lip and close my eyes momentarily as I feel him inching his way in. Pain becomes illicit pleasure, dizzying in its power. "Oh, God."

Gently, he pulls out his finger, kisses my lower back, flips me over, and covers my body with his. "Like this."

Holding my arms above my head with his hands, I wrap my legs around his waist as he enters me in one swift, deep thrust. His punishing hardness fills me to the hilt, making me cry in ecstasy. By now my need for him doesn't burn—it sears through me.

But as he continues to take me, his hips pumping in and out of me, the familiar sense of unworthiness whenever I'm with him comes over me. The only difference this time is that *I know* I'm not worthy of him.

"Why me, Ronan?" I ask, grabbing his ass and pulling him deeper inside of me. The penetration so intense, I moan, feeling dizzy.

He stops thrusting, his pulsating cock buried inside me. "Because when I look at you, I see everything I want and everything I need."

And then he proceeds to fuck the living daylights out of me.

"What are you doing over there?" I hear Ronan ask in a sleepy voice. "Come back to me. The bed still smells like you."

I'm sitting on his chair by the window when he wakes up. I turn around to find a naked Ronan on his back, rubbing his eyes with the palms of his hands. His wavy hair sticking out in every direction possible screams sex. I smile, pulling my legs closer to my chest, and shake my head no, looking out the window again.

I watch the early morning sun bathe buildings and the streets in light while people go about their business, ready to start their day. My eyes follow a couple walking, and I feel such despairing sadness come over me, erasing any trace of a smile off my face.

And I know why …

I grab a piece of my hair and begin braiding. "I'm just looking at the city … isn't it so dazzling, so free, so uninhibited?"

"I'll show you free and uninhibited, baby."

I slant my eyes in his direction, memorizing the way he's looking at me, memorizing the way it feels to be with him. But when our gazes connect we break into laughter, filling the room with fleeting happiness.

With the laughter dying, leaving what feels like the beginning of a gap between us, Ronan sobers up, and adds, his voice like liquid velvet, "Come here, baby. I need you."

"Nu-uh. I know what you want and I'm tired," I lie.

"If you don't get your cute little ass back here, I'm coming to get you."

I want to tell him to come and get me, but I'm afraid that my voice will betray me, so I just shake my head and continue to stare out the window, braiding my hair. Before I know it, a hand is reaching for mine, helping me to stand up, and I'm enveloped in a choking embrace. Without saying a word, I bury my face in his chest, feeling his skin soft as silk against my cheek, and breathe in his smell. I can also hear the beating of his heart, and like a lullaby it helps to soothe me. After a couple of minutes pass by in silence, our breathing the only sound in the room, Ronan places a hand under my chin and makes me look at him.

"I got something for you."

"You did? Why?"

He lets me go, walking toward his nightstand. "Just because." He retrieves a package and makes his way back to me.

"Because why? How?"

He smiles an impish smile that makes him look so much younger than he is. "Just open it, Blaire."

The memory of what it felt like kissing Lawrence flashes through my mind. "But I don't deserve it."

"Let's agree to disagree on that, shall we?"

"But—"

"Shh. Will you stop being so stubborn for once and just let me give you something?"

I purse my lips as I stare at him with daggers in my eyes. "I hate you sometimes, you know?"

Ronan laughs out loud. "Yeah, keep telling yourself that."

I'm about to tell him he's so full of himself when he raises his hand. "Nope. I won't hear it. Open the gift first, then you can continue telling me how much you hate me."

"You suck."

I look down at the small package in my hands, the wrapping paper a soft purple. Smiling, I unwrap the gift, and as the paper falls on the floor completely forgotten, I uncover a Hello Kitty watch. The beating of my heart comes to a full stop as I stare at the dial. There's an ache in my chest and butterflies in my stomach.

"You remembered," I whisper softly.

It's not the same as the one I wanted my parents to get me—it's better. This is probably the most unassuming and least expensive gift I've ever received, but as my vision begins to blur from tears, I know that it's priceless.

My hands trembling, I stare at the gift when I feel his hand under my chin, gently tipping it up until our eyes meet. And the way he's looking at me …

Oh, the way he's looking at me is what love poems are written about.

"How could I forget?" he says softly.

My chest is full of emotions—good, bad, and confusing. It feels as though it might burst with the intensity of it all. And if I had any questions as to whether I was falling for him or not, they are completely answered at this moment.

I am.

Hard.

I look up as I fight the tears that threaten to spill over, ready to thank him, but the words get stuck in my throat.

"Damn. My purpose of giving you that watch was to see you smile, not make you cry."

He reaches for the watch, but I slap his hand away and cradle the gift close to my chest. "Don't even think about it! I love it."

"Then what made you look so sad?"

"No … it wasn't that. It's just the nicest thing anyone has ever given me." I pause, losing myself in his eyes. "Thank you, Ronan. Thank you so much."

"Here, let me put it on you."

Ronan takes the gift away from my hands and puts the watch on my wrist.

"So you really like it?"

As I stare at his gift, memories of my childhood, of broken dreams, and of the past few weeks spent with him swirl in my head: Ronan, my parents, happiness and heartache, tears and laughter, loneliness and companionship.

The memory of a particular dream I used to have all the time as a little girl fleets back, flooding my entire being with physical pain. In that dream, I'm holding my mom's hands as we spin in circles as fast as our legs would allow us. The speed of our bodies propelled us to go faster and faster with each turn, while colors and shapes became a blurred rainbow around us. Careless and free, we threw our heads back laughing as hard as the forever young—the easy moment feeling magical. I shouldn't have been able to see my dad, but because it was a dream, I knew he was watching us. Reclined lazily against a tree, a smile on his attractive face, he didn't look drunk as he usually did. Instead, his clothes were immaculate, his black hair smoothed to the side. But it was what I saw in his blue eyes that I loved the most. They sparkled with love for both his wife and daughter. And at that moment, when our eyes connected, my mom's sweet laugh filling my ears, I knew I was loved.

I knew I was loved.

But then I would wake up, finding myself on a cold bed in an empty room. I would touch my cheeks and find that they were wet because I was crying in my dreams.

Again.

So as I continue to stare at the watch that Ronan gave me, I lose what little composure I have left and break down completely.

But a part of me wonders ...

Is love really so bad?

Is wanting something as beautiful and simple as love such an awful thing?

It must be because it hurts. My chest hurts. My heart hurts. The beauty of this is driving me fucking insane. What will happen to me when this ends? Maybe before today, I could have walked away from him unscathed, but I don't think that's possible anymore. I can't continue lying to myself. I'm falling for him, and because of that, it has to come to an end.

I can't help the hysterical half laugh, half sob that escapes my mouth.

"I'm sorry ... I need a moment," I say, pushing Ronan away and running to the bathroom.

I'm drying my face with a tissue when I feel Ronan come up behind me. He grabs me by the arm and spins me around so we're face to face.

"Why are you crying?" he asks as his thumb touches some of the moisture left from my tears on my cheeks. "What's the matter, babe?"

I shake my head. "What are you doing with me, Ronan? You're too good for me. You should be with someone who doesn't have so much fucking baggage. Someone who will be able to give herself completely to you. You do something nice for me and I break down and cry. Don't you see how fucked up I am? I'm not right for you. I don't deserve you. I don't deserve you."

I keep repeating myself over and over again, hoping that I'll make him believe those words, and convince my heart that this is over.

But Ronan won't listen to me. Pulling me into an embrace, he says, "Shhh ... You deserve me and I'm not going anywhere."

I speak into his chest. "You shouldn't. I'm—"

"Yeah, yeah, you keep saying that you're not worthy of me and that you're so fucked up. But you know what? I don't fucking care. I don't want perfect—I don't need it. I just want you, Blaire. I just want you. Look at me!"

I raise my face and drown in the depths of his warm eyes.

"One day you're going to let me love you, and I'm going to hold you so tight I'll never let you go. I'm going to love you as if it were the one thing I was meant to do. As if it were my purpose in life. Don't you see it, Blaire? Don't you get it? You're in me. In everything I see. In everything I touch. You're in the air I breathe, in the water I drink, and in every dream I dream. I want to tell you so much more, but I know that you're not ready to hear it."

Listening to his words, wanting to believe them, wanting to make them real is what makes me realize that it's over. *I can't.* These feelings will destroy me. They already have. I'm numb from the inside out as I recognize that our halcyon days have come to an end.

Ronan cups my face in his hands. "We'll be okay. I promise you, Blaire." He seals the space between us with the first of our last kisses. However, this time I don't get lost in the dance of our tongues and the feel of his hands gliding across my skin. This time, when he guides me to his bed and we become one on top of his sheets, I fake my climax. It's like my body knows what my conscience hasn't admitted yet. It feels ... final.

And as he comes inside me, his body shaking on top of mine, it's not the words he whispers in my ear that I hear. They aren't the ones spinning inside my head—they are Lawrence's.

He was right.

chapter eighteen.

Later that night ...

LIKE THE COWARD I AM, I WAIT UNTIL I'm sure that Ronan has fallen asleep to get out of bed and put my clothes on.

The numbness remains. There are no tears to be shed. I'm cold to the bone, but I'm finally at peace. I thought that I wouldn't be able to tear myself away from Ronan, but oddly enough, it's quite easy. I went from feeling so much, to feeling nothing at all.

I'm empty. Hollow.

After I grab my bag, I walk toward the bed and stop to watch him sleep, his brown hair partially covering his eyes. A part of me wants to lie down next to him and hold onto his body as if it were my anchor and get lost in his beauty. I want to run my fingers across his hair, feeling its softness one last time, but I don't. I've lost that right.

And isn't that how life works, after all? All good things in life never last. Like a good high, at some point you must come down and crash and burn. Things end. People break unspoken promises. People break hearts. People move on and forget.

After a while, I put my bag down by the foot of the bed and remove his gift from my wrist. As I take off the watch, I feel as though I'm ripping my heart out from my chest.

I place the watch on his nightstand, lean down and give him one last kiss. "Good-bye, my sweet, sweet boy."

Straightening, I pick up my bag and run my hands over my wrinkled skirt. Dispassionately, I notice my hands shaking, but I still turn on my heel and walk out of his room, his apartment.

Out of his life.

Fear is a prison. A feeling of crippling power that spreads darkness within. It blinds. It questions. It takes over every decision we make, coloring it with doubt. Fear, for most of us, rules our lives, and it's only when you conquer it that you can truly live your life to the fullest.

However, fear isn't a bad thing. Because fear prevents me from getting hurt over and over again—from being careless with my emotions. And it's the same fear that propels me to ignore Ronan's calls and not answer his texts for the next two days. I delete every single text and voice message without opening them.

And it's that same fear that drives me to walk over to my vanity, grab the business card propped against a perfume bottle, pick up my phone and give Lawrence a call. Dismissing Ronan and memories of our halcyon days once and for all.

Yes, fear is not all that bad.

chapter nineteen.

WORRYING MY LIP AND CHIPPING away the gunmetal polish from my nails, I wait for the man who has been in the periphery of my thoughts to answer the call. I feel short of breath. My hands are sweating. The beating of my heart escalates with each ring of the connecting call, bringing him closer to me, but there's no dread, no panic—just acceptance.

With Ronan, I thought happiness could be attainable, almost within my grasp. And it was for a while. But love is never enough, is it? And really, what did I expect? A tiger can't change its stripes. Even if I hadn't ended it, how long before the reality of who I am, of what I want in a man—what I seek—became a burden? How long would it be before Ronan realized I was just a beautiful shell with nothing inside but an echo of my former self? I don't want love since I have no need for it. I don't want to feel. I want everything that money can buy, even if it's at the expense of my soul, or whatever is left of it anyway.

A memory of a smiling Ronan on our first date flashes through my mind.

"Go out with me, Blaire."
I shake my head, fighting a smile. "I know I'm going to regret this."

"Maybe … but why not? Live a little."

"I don't want to. I like my life to be planned and uncomplicated."

"It's better to live a life full of regrets than not live at all." Lowering his voice, he adds huskily, *"Let me show you how it's done."*

I close my eyes and tighten my hold on the cell. *No. No. No.* I won't let him do this to me. I won't let him and the memory of his sweet words prevent me from reaching my goals. If I've had any small and lingering doubt that I made the wrong choice by leaving him, this reinforces my decision.

After five or six rings without an answer, I'm about to hang up when he picks up. "Hello," is all he says in that toe curling and delicious voice of his.

I grip the phone harder. "It's me. Tell me when to meet you and I'll be there."

"Good girl. You won't regret it."

"Wait!"

"Yes?" He sounds amused.

"I want a lot of money."

"That's fine. I have more than enough."

After he tells me to expect a call from his assistant, Gina, to finalize the details of the date, I hang up without saying another word. There's no need. I've already made up my mind, and once I do, I never change it.

I'm about to put my phone away when I see an alert for a new message from Ronan. Without bothering to open and read it, I reply.

    B: I don't want complicated. Please don't
    contact me again.

And he doesn't.

chapter twenty.

AM I REALLY GOING TO DO IT?

Can I possibly go through with this?

I step closer to the mirror and grab a chunk of my black hair. I tug. Hard. As hard as the men who fuck me pull it. It makes me want to throw up. But I like this, right? I watch the way my blue eyes sparkle feverishly as I pull harder, making myself wince, and think to myself that there is no difference. Well ... yes. There is one. Instead of gifts or living rent free for a couple of months because the guy I'm screwing has it covered, I'm going to actually get paid for my *services* and then *ta-ta,* see you never.

And that's exactly what I want.

Especially after ...

I can't even bring myself to say his name.

I watch indecision reflect in my eyes, but I shake it off like I've shaken off every single kind of emotion that comes close to making me feel. I don't want to feel anything. I can't. Feeling is bad. It leaves you vulnerable. And I don't have time for emotions like guilt or shame.

I like money.

I like power.

I like adoration.

I like sex.

I'm good at it, or so the guys I have screwed tell me. Maybe looking pretty and being someone's fuck toy is all I'm good at. But hey, I can't complain because that's all me. My fault. My choice. And it's not like I'm the first gold digger to ever spread her legs for the right amount of money.

I just wish the nausea would go away.

I turn around and head toward my bed, leaving a mirror full of lies behind. I put on the tiniest black thong I own, grab the deep red bandage dress lying on top of my duvet and slip it on. As the dress goes down, I feel the way the silk begins to constrict my body as it covers more areas of me, and I love it.

I walk to my bathroom and finish putting my makeup on. Tonight, I want to steal Lawrence's breath away, so I take my time with my usual ritual. I want to look my best when I kill what little innocence and beauty I have left inside of me, and what better way to do it than by burning as bright as a star.

I fluff my hair and watch the way it covers most of my back, like a shiny black river. I take a step back and take a look at myself. Smiling into my reflection, I notice the way my smile doesn't reach my eyes. How empty and cold they look.

My mask is on.

"Excuse me."

"Yes, miss?" the chauffer responds.

"I was wondering where exactly in Long Island are you taking me?"

I'm riding in the black Rolls Royce that Lawrence sent to pick me up and bring me to him. I know that the air conditioner is on in the car, but I feel like I'm standing next to an open fire I'm so hot.

"I'm driving you to his estate—Rothschild Hall. It's located in Center Island, miss."

"He lives in a place that has a name? That big, huh?" I ask, my voice ringing with sarcasm. But I guess I should believe him. Only houses that pretty much have their own zip code forgo a number for a name. I've been to a few summer parties in those kinds of places.

The driver chuckles, our eyes connecting in the rearview mirror. "You could say that."

"I'm Blaire, by the way. What's your name?"

The man with skin the color of cinnamon smiles. "I'm Tony."

"Nice meeting you, Tony."

"Nice meeting you, Miss Blaire."

"Oh, God, I'm no miss," I say, winking at him saucily. "Just call me Blaire, please."

The corner of his lip twitches. "Sure, Blaire."

We're just getting out of the Midtown Tunnel when I ask, "So how long have you been working for Lawrence?"

"I've worked for the Rothschild family for the last thirty years, but the years are beginning to take a toll on me, so I now only drive Laurie—I mean, Mr. Rothschild a couple of days a week."

"Laurie?" It's hard to imagine that the virile man I met at the museum could be called Laurie. It makes me want to giggle.

"He hates to be called by that name. Ever since he was a little imp of six," he says, laughter and love blended in his voice.

We chat about his family, but the conversation comes to a halt when he asks about mine. The question reminds me of why I'm in this car on my way to meet his boss. It reminds me of who I am and of my past. And amusingly enough, the memory that comes to mind is one of my first days in the big city soon after I turned eighteen and left my hometown. I was able to get a job as a waitress at an Italian restaurant on Wall Street. I suspect I only got the position because of my looks, since I had no prior work experience.

He was one of the regulars, like they always are. A little older than Mr. Callahan and with a cosmopolitan air about him, he impressed me. He kept coming back, sometimes with friends, sometimes alone. But he always came back. He always matched my tip with the bill. He always made sure I knew how wealthy he was. When I gave him my phone number, I got flowers. When I accepted his first invitation to go to dinner, I got spoiled with gifts. When I finally accepted his overtures ...

As my high heels glide across the glossy floor, I spot him sitting by the bar. A man in his mid-forties wearing jeans, a crisp white button down and a navy sports jacket with leather loafers, glances my way and immediately stands up. His smile vacant, his eyes starved.

Time to act the part. Time to play Blaire. Time to play myself.

Slowly, I make eye contact, letting the blue of my eyes hypnotize him while I smile seductively. It's a smile that will let him imagine how my mouth will look wrapped around his cock. And it's working. The way his eyes devour me makes my pulse race. There's nothing more deliciously intoxicating than adulation.

When I'm standing in front of him, I extend my hand toward him. "Hi, Luke," I say breathlessly.

"Blaire ... you look exquisite tonight," he murmurs.

The smell of his expensive cologne tickles my nose and the back of my throat. Did the man shower in it? It makes me want to throw up.

"Would you like a drink before we go upstairs?"

I want to pat him on the knee and coo, "Calm down, doggie, calm down," but I can't, so I smile.

"Sure. A glass of champagne, please."

Maybe if I get drunk enough, I won't have to feel his hands and mouth on me. I won't have to feel him moving inside of me.

Could I be so lucky?

For a fraction of a second, I wonder if he realizes I'm only eighteen, but I guess it doesn't matter. He probably likes me because I look so young.

After two rounds of drinks, scotch on the rocks for him and champagne for me, he leans closer to me, grabs my ass, and murmurs in my ear, "No more alcohol for you. I've waited for a long time to do this, and I want you lucid."

"Let's get out of here then," I say as I fight the part of me that wants to run away from this place, never turning back. But this is what I came for. I have to learn how to play this game. My survival depends on it.

He wraps a muscular arm around my waist and leads the way to the elevator. Once the doors close behind us, Luke pins me against the wall and begins kissing my neck and the top curve of my breasts. His lips are soft and smooth as they leave wet traces along the grooves of my exposed body. Closing my eyes—and mind—numbing myself to feeling and emotion, I tip my head back and allow him to get his money's worth.

Inside his hotel room, I ask, "Now what?"

"Now I get to do what I've wanted to do all night," he says as he kisses me on the mouth. Lying me on the bed, he pushes my hair to the side and lets his fingers linger on my face, his touch scalding my skin.

"You're so beautiful ... the most beautiful woman I've ever seen," he whispers, his hands groping me everywhere.

I can see myself reflected in his eyes and my reflection scares me. As he speaks words that Mr. Callahan muttered before, I keep looking at my reflection. How cold and empty do I look ... but beautiful, always beautiful.

He doesn't bother taking my dress off before he lifts the skirt to my waist, unzips his pants, rolls a condom on his already hard cock, and pushes inside me. I'm not wet so it hurts a little, but the more he pushes and plays with my clit, the more my body fights my disgust. The more it wants it.

As he continues to thrust, I picture everything I want: the easy life, the best of everything, security. I tell myself that as long as I let him fuck me and not think about it, I can have it all.

I'm about to close my eyes and turn my cheek to the side, when I hear him say, "Don't. I want to see your face."

So I don't. I watch his red and sweaty face as he fucks me. I memorize every sound, every smell, every grunt, and every soiled kiss. I repeat over and over again that this is what I want until the words don't sound so hollow in my ears.

When he pulls out, I hate to see that he's covered in my body's response to him. And when he goes down on me, I can't help but moan when I feel the wet softness of his tongue licking my clit, sucking it and biting it between his teeth. I don't want to like it. I want to be disgusted, and I am, but my body can't lie to me. It won't lie to me. My body likes the way this man is fucking me. On the outside, I moan and pant because it's me, but on the inside ... on the inside I'm dying a slow death with each thrust.

But I don't care.

This is me taking control of my life. This is me becoming whatever I need to be in order to achieve my goals. And, most importantly, I don't care because when this is over, all my sins will be paid for.

Very well.

Besides, he promised to take me apartment hunting tomorrow morning, because his lovely Blaire needs a place of her own.

"We're here, Miss," I hear him say, bringing me back to the present.

I shake the memories and forget about Luke. That man turned out to be a pig. He gave me all the money I needed to live more than comfortably, but he had a thing for forgetting the meaning of the word *no* after one too many drinks.

We leave the tall iron gates behind and drive for a while, past opulent green lawns and majestic trees until a large house comes into view. I'm surprised by how beautiful it is. It's not as big as I expected but still very impressive.

"Oh my God. It's perfect," I say as I stare at the Victorian home with its picturesque windows and thick columns made out of marble. The house must have at least twenty rooms.

I hear Tony chuckle.

"What's so funny?" I'm afraid to have sounded naïve or green. *Oh, the horror.*

"That's only the guesthouse, Miss Blaire."

"O-Only?" I ask, my voice breaking.

"Yes. Just one moment ... The Hall is coming up."

I stare ahead as he drives for another couple of minutes, truly nervous for the first time since we've left my apartment.

"And *that*, Miss Blaire, is Rothschild Hall," he says, beaming with pride when a house (more like a damn castle) that would put Oprah's to shame comes into view. It's splendid.

"Whoa."

What the fuck did I get myself into?

I might just be out of my league this time.

chapter **twenty-one.**

THE GRAND OAK DOORS OPEN.

The Rolls Royce parks next to the steps leading to the main entrance and the welcoming lights coming from inside illuminate the darkness around us. Once Tony lets me out of the car, I'm engulfed in the warmth and mugginess of the night.

"Have a lovely evening," Tony says as I watch an older man dressed in a striking black suit step outside and wait for me, observing me closely.

"Thank you, Tony." I smile. I'm about to ask him if he'll be the one to drive me back to the city when I'm ready to leave, but I don't. I'm not exactly sure what will happen tonight; if I'll leave after a couple of hours or if I'm supposed to spend the night. *Maybe Lawrence expects a trial fuck—or a couple—before sealing the deal?* I shrug. It doesn't matter one way or another.

As I climb up the steps, a cool breeze blows past me, kissing my bare arms and legs. It provokes a delicious feeling within me. I've almost reached the landing when a prickle of awareness makes me lift my gaze to the second floor right above the open doors. I expect to find someone standing there, but the window is empty; nothing but a warm glow coming from the inside is visible. I rub the back of my neck, dismissing the feeling of being watched, but the small hairs on my arms stand on end.

"Good evening, Miss White. I'm William, Mr. Rothschild's Butler. If you would be so kind as to follow me, Mr. Rothschild is waiting for you in the library," the older gentleman says gravely.

"Hello there," I say cheekily. Something about his serious expression compels me to try and make him smile. Sadly, it doesn't work. Sighing, I let my eyes survey my surroundings. I don't want to be impressed. I don't want to feel awestruck by the grandeur of this house. I really wish I could rub it off as something I've seen hundreds of times before, and maybe in a way I have, but nothing on this scale. Staring ahead as I wait for William to close the doors behind me, I take in the black marble staircase that splits in two at the bottom. My gaze follows its length until my eyes land on the crystal chandelier hanging from the cathedral ceiling. If that thing were to fall on someone, it would crush him to death. It's enormous, and absolutely radiant. The paintings lining the entrance hall alone must be worth a queen's ransom. With a quick glance, I'm able to recognize a Picasso, a Frida Kahlo, and a Dali. Except for the Frida, who's Mexican, you can say that Lawrence has a thing for Spanish artists.

Doing a 360-degree turn, I absorb the red roses and orchids in enormous crystal vases and the gleaming white and black marble floor. I hear someone cough, making me realize that I'm gawking. I shake my head.

I've got this. This is nothing new. Just another man, just another day.

Yet the beating of my heart only gets louder, and the butterflies creating chaos within me only get rowdier with every step that I make, with every step that brings me closer to him. My body never lies—I'm nervous. Crazy enough, I've forgotten what he looks like except for the color of his eyes. His calm and vacant eyes that remind me of money. The eyes I forgot all about while dreaming a little dream with a brown-eyed boy.

Curling my hands into fists, I'm angry with myself because Ronan isn't supposed to usurp my thoughts. He's supposed to be a thing of the past. And he will be. Even if it's the last thing I do.

When we stand in front of the double doors, I watch William rap on the door twice. Not a minute goes by before I hear *him* order loud and clear, "Come in." An unforgettable voice with the power to make the bravest of men quake in their shoes fills my ears.

"Hello, Blaire."

I watch William quietly close the door behind us.

All alone now, I turn to face Lawrence, who's watching me closely, an indecipherable expression on his face.

"Please, sit down," he says.

"Thank you." I walk toward a chocolate brown leather sofa.

Once I sit down, I stare at him, expecting him to start a conversation, but he doesn't. As a matter of fact, he just stands there looking at me. I get the feeling that he wants to get under my skin, but I sure as hell won't let that happen, so I just return his stare. But as the uncomfortable silence in the room stretches for thirty seconds, a minute, two minutes ...

I laugh.

A deep chuckle escapes my lips, and it feels so fucking good. The sound cuts through the tension in the room.

A cool Lawrence places his hands behind his back and continues to stare at me. "May I ask what you find so amusing?"

"I feel like I'm stuck in the most bizarre dream. Some parts are Pretty Woman and others Pride and Prejudice, which is pretty funny if you think about it. It's like having Julia's character going to Pemberley Hall for a quick fuck."

He raises an eyebrow, his lips twitching. "Poor Darcy. I think the fellow could do better than a quick fuck." He moves to sit in the love seat across from me.

"You know who Darcy is?" I ask surprised.

"Many years around women have rubbed off on me," he says sardonically.

I laugh. "I feel bad for Jane. She must be rolling in her grave for my comparison."

"You don't say."

I shrug. "But it's true. Ever since Tony came to pick me up in a Rolls Royce early in the evening … your house, I mean *Rothschild Hall* … the gardens … William … the Picasso and Kahlo"—I look him in the eye—"you."

Lawrence nods, amusement making his eyes twinkle in the dimly lit room. "So besides knowing art and light-hearted Hollywood films, you know Jane Austen—"

"Faithfully. I mean, there wouldn't be a Clueless without an Emma."

"How interesting. Attractive and smart—a deadly combination."

Without breaking eye contact, I tilt my head to the side and grin impertinently. "And you're handsome and loaded. An even deadlier one."

That earns me a smile. An achingly beautiful smile that changes his features from handsome to devastating. As we continue to stare at each other, amusement slowly fading from our faces, the friendly atmosphere dissolves like smoke in the air and an erotic tension fills the space between us. I lick my lips and notice the way his suddenly very dark eyes follow the motion of my tongue. Is he picturing it wrapped around his cock? Is he picturing me on my knees as he sits on that leather loveseat, my head in his lap while I fuck him with my mouth?

The moment is broken when someone knocks on the door before opening it and letting themself in.

"Dinner is ready, Mr. Rothschild," we hear William say.

"Thank you. You may leave us now, William," he says, looking toward the door.

He felt it too. I let out a shaky breath and watch him run a hand through his hair. Lawrence turns, composed and detached once again, and addresses me. "Would you like to continue our conversation in the dining room instead?"

"Sure." I stand up. The slow burn between my legs is yet to be extinguished. As I collect myself, I take a moment to look around for the first time since I walked in the library. Everywhere I look there are rows upon rows of mahogany bookshelves filled with leather-bound tomes, shiny hardcovers, or used paperbacks—a treasure within one's reach.

"Wow ... now *this* is what I call a library. I think this room rivals my love of Barneys New York shoe floor."

I turn in his direction and watch an amused Lawrence rise from his sitting position. A half smile graces his manly face as he makes his way toward me, his step sure and firm. I raise an eyebrow and cross my arms on my chest.

"What's so funny?"

He doesn't answer my question. Instead, he keeps walking until he's standing in front of me. He's so close I can smell the spicy undertones of his cologne and I can see the dark stubble contouring the strong lines of his jaw. If I wanted to, I could place my hands on his chest and feel his heartbeat. *I wonder if it's as fast as mine?*

The temperature in the room feels as though it has spiked a couple of degrees. "Aren't you going to say something?" I ask.

Pinning me with his gaze, he takes another step until the space between us is completely nonexistent. I take a deep breath and let it out shakily. "*Okay*, I guess no—"

He places a finger on my mouth, silencing me. We eye one other as he untangles my hands and guides them behind my back, holding them prisoner there. Captivated under his gaze, I can feel the ends of my hair grazing our skin. My head spins the instant the tip of his nose begins to trace the curve of my jaw ever so gently ... the length of my neck. His touch is everywhere, engulfing me.

"How beautiful you are," he murmurs against my skin.

I swallow hard. "Thank you."

"No, don't thank me. I wasn't giving you a compliment. I was stating a fact."

"Well, in that case ... I guess, I already knew that."

When he pulls slightly back, his eyes hooded with desire, I think he's going to kiss me. Instinctively, I close my eyes, stand on my tiptoes, and wait, expecting his lips to touch mine, but nothing happens. Instead, I feel the tickling sensation of his breath behind my ear, before he whispers, "Tell me, Blaire ... what happened to that special someone?"

Again, I find myself unable to lie to him. "He made me feel too much."

"So why aren't you with him if he made you feel that way?"

"That's exactly why. He made me feel things. Made me *yearn* for things that I don't want. Things that I don't need."

"And me, Blaire? What do I make you feel?" He runs the back of his fingers along my collarbone.

"You make me feel nothing, which is everything."

"Do you love him?"

"Would it make a difference if I did?"

He's quiet, seemingly waging his answer. "No. Not at all."

After a quick tour of the place, we arrive at the grand dining room, and the first thing I notice is the lemony smell that permeates the air from the perfectly polished parquet floor. As we make our way to the head of a rectangular dining table, I don't bother to admire the wood covered walls with their intricate carvings, or the Chinese landscape paintings. Instead, I direct all of my attention to the man walking next to me.

He is wearing a pair of dark denim jeans that sit perfectly on his hips and a light blue button down with the top two buttons unfastened. The hue of the shirt accentuates the color of his skin and the rich dark brown of his hair. It's easy to see why he's considered a ruthless man, in and out of bed. After spending no more than thirty minutes in his presence, I can sense that there is an animal, a very dangerous predator hiding underneath the expensive and civilized clothes he wears. There is an untamed wildness about him. He is mystery and darkness, and I have an inkling that many a woman before me has fallen for the illusion that she could be the one to tame him, only to be disappointed when she fails miserably.

As I wait for dessert to arrive, I look at the man sitting to my left. He's watching me as well, appraising me. He also happens to look as appealing and delicious as that glass of red wine in his hand.

"What are you thinking about? You seem distracted," I hear him say, bringing me out of my reverie.

"I don't know … just meaningless stuff, really. You have an enchanting home, by the way."

"Thank you."

I reach for my glass of wine and take a sip. "You're a man of few words, aren't you? I haven't shut up since we sat down to eat and you've barely said more than two words."

"Really? I hadn't noticed," he says sarcastically, his eyes twinkling.

"Okay, maybe that was an exaggeration, but you get my meaning."

"There's not much to say that you probably haven't already read on the Internet."

I laugh. "Guilty as charged. It was probably the first thing I did."

That earns me a smile—a sinful smile that shouldn't feel as though it's crawling under my skin, leaving a trace of heat behind, but it does. It definitely does.

"It's quite all right. Besides, I enjoy listening to you talk. I find it … refreshing."

"Yeah, right. I'm probably putting you to sleep. Anyway, you know what they say …"

"No, why don't you enlighten me?"

I smirk. "It's the quiet ones you have to be careful with. They have the dirtiest minds."

He roars with laughter, and somehow that makes me happy. Once he's calmed down, he drains his wine in one gulp, places the glass on the table, and turns to look at me, amusement dancing in his green eyes.

"I'm not a saint, Blaire. I've lived my life fully and had more than a few indulgences along the way."

"Good because I'm no angel."

"Come here, Blaire, let me take a look at you," he says, his voice growing husky.

I take another sip of wine as we eye each other, making the moment stretch a little longer. The way he's now staring at me—all traces of laughter gone—unnerves me, but I won't cower in front of him. If anything, it makes me want to make him uncomfortable in return. I want to watch him lose his cool.

Once I return my glass to the table, I wipe the corners of my lips with the cloth napkin that was on my lap and place it next to my spoon before I stand.

When he realizes that I plan to sit on the table in front of him, he pushes his chair slightly back to give me the space I need. Once I'm seated, we face each other silently, each daring the other to finally cross the line we've been skirting all night and acknowledge that this isn't some sort of romantic date. *Quite the contrary.*

"Go ahead." I spread my legs as wide as the tight skirt of my dress will allow. "Take a look." I place one hand on the cool wood underneath me for support, and use my free hand to pull my black thong to the side, completely baring myself to him. "Tell me, Lawrence … do you like what you see?"

He's quiet as he takes *all* of me in. His breathing doesn't catch. His eyes, though dark with desire, don't hesitate to boldly peruse my body. He remains calmly seated in the high-back wooden chair as I brazenly expose myself to him. I should be ashamed—embarrassed—but instead, pure and unadulterated excitement runs through my veins, making my body hum with an illicit kind of thrill. The man is a taboo … forbidden, yet so appealing.

After several seconds, *or an eternity*, he stands between my legs, the chair making a scratching sound as he pushes it back. He strokes my upper thigh with the back of his hand ever so gently. Higher and higher his touch invades, assaulting my senses until it's dangerously close to my entrance.

"Tell me, Blaire. Why do you think you're here?" he asks nonchalantly as I watch his hand finally slide between my thighs, spreading me open with two of his fingers. I can feel the roughness of his jeans caressing the inside of my thighs when he steps closer to me.

I'm about to answer him when I feel his middle finger flick my clit, rubbing it in nice slow circles. I suppress a moan. "I'm here because *I* have something *you* want, and *you* have something *I* want."

"Spread your legs wider," he orders and I follow. "You're correct. I want to sleep with you for as long as I'm in New York. No strings attached, no feelings, no complications. And, Blaire, I'm willing to pay whatever you ask as long as you don't forget those basic and simple rules."

"I won't, but what happens after?"

"You walk away with a full bank account."

Then he slips one … two … three fingers inside me, thrusting evenly, coating his fingers in my body's reaction to his touch. Pumping in and out, fingering me on a table that probably costs more than two months of my rent.

"You're so responsive," he says, withdrawing his damp fingers. He brings them inside his mouth and sucks them clean. I watch the flash of his tongue as he drags them out, my taste leaving a trace behind.

I swallow hard when he returns his three fingers to my entrance and starts impaling me with his hand, forcing me to feel every single inch as they leave my body only to be driven back with more force than before. A part of me wants to hate his touch, wants to be disgusted with his proposition, but I would only be fooling myself. The real Blaire, the one who rules my decisions, fucking loves it.

"What do you say, Blaire?" I hear him ask hoarsely, his voice finally giving him up. He's as affected as I am.

I moan, my body tight with pleasure and tension. My head swirls in a haze of lust. I'm a wanton woman at his feet, and I don't care. As I watch his glistening fingers disappearing between my legs, I pant, "But what about love, Lawrence? Don't you want my love too?"

"No. Save that for your infinite conquests," he says, the pad of his thumb now rubbing my clit mercilessly while he continues to finger-fuck me, driving me closer to blissful hell. "Or that special someone you talked about."

I gasp, placing a hand on his shoulder for support. I'm so close to coming ... the colors in the room become brighter, my senses heightened. I don't know why I asked that question. We understand each other perfectly: we use and we discard.

He drives harder and harder and harder until my release hits me with the blinding power of thunder. A bodily frenzy takes over as I come undone from the inside out. My body drained from such a powerful climax, I open my eyes to find him watching me closely. The crests of his cheeks flushed, his hair still perfect, but the spark in his eyes burns so brightly, so vividly, I can feel it searing a hole through me. He leans forward as he pulls out and runs his wet fingers over my lips. I can smell myself on him, and if I wanted to, I could taste myself on his fingertips.

"If love is what you seek, I suggest we finish dinner and pretend this conversation never happened. Let me keep your memory alive by not regretting having met you and being disillusioned with reality. I would rather remember you as the strikingly beautiful woman with the hunger in her eyes who didn't care for plebeian feelings such as love."

"No need for that. I don't want any of those things either. Love ruins everything."

"Good. So what do you say, Blaire? Will it be a yes ... or a no?"

"I'll need a lot of money. I want a flat in SoHo with my name on its deed." I grin. "I want to be spoiled rotten."

"Of course. I'll give you that and more."

"Just one more question."

He smiles, appearing to have expected that. "Yes?"

"Why choose me when you could be with anyone? Someone famous and more beautiful?"

"More beautiful than you? I doubt it."

"Really?" I raise an eyebrow sardonically and purse my lips, which makes him laugh.

Quiet for a moment as the room becomes a blur around us, he focuses his gaze on me and runs a hand through my long hair. "You're too smart for your own good, Blaire. You know that, right? But fine. It's because we speak the same language. You and me ... we're cut from the same cloth. We see something we want and we take it. We don't let emotions get the better of us."

What do I have to lose? If I'm honest with myself, this is my dream come true. No feelings. No emotions. Just sex, and a shit load of money.

"Okay," I swallow once, "make me an offer."

"Name a sum."

I chew the inside of my lip, not sure how far to push him, but then I remember I have nothing to lose. Besides, I can tell that he really wants me. "Do you have a piece of paper?"

Amusement lights up his eyes. "Why? Don't tell me you're feeling shy, Blaire?"

I huff, but rise to his challenge nonetheless. "Fine. I'll tell you."

"There ... that's the Blaire I know and like."

I hold up one finger. "Start adding the zeros, my friend."

"Ten thousand."

Smiling impishly, I shake my head. "Come on, you can do better than that," I tease.

"A hundred thousand."

"Higher," I say and make him chuckle.

"A million."

I nod and feel as though I just gambled a fortune away on blackjack. "I want a million per month, for however long you need me. *And* that doesn't include the apartment."

"It's yours."

"That's it?" I ask incredulously. "You're giving me that much money just like that?"

"Yes, why not? I've told you I want you. And I always get what I want."

Before I leave for the night, we come back to the library to grab my clutch. After I retrieve it from the same brown sofa where I sat earlier in the night, I turn to look at him. He's standing by the entryway with his hands in the front pockets of his jeans, his shoulder propped casually against the open door. Looking calm and almost bored, it's hard to imagine that this is the same man who just fucked me raw with his fingers on his dining room table.

"Are you sure you don't want me to, um, return the favor? Isn't that part of the deal?" I ask, thinking that it's funny how things between us can go from purely sexual to friendly—almost as if nothing has happened.

He cups the back of his neck, rubbing it. "Not tonight, Blaire. Go home, sleep on our agreement, and call me tomorrow to let me know your final decision."

"Why? You don't think I can make sound decisions in the throes of ecstasy?" I mock.

He chuckles once. "Frankly, Blaire, I couldn't care less. But the next time we see each other I plan to fuck you until you don't know whether you're begging me to stop or begging me to fuck you harder. Until the hours cease to exist and the only thing

162

that matters is total surrender. I plan on putting that beautiful and brazen mouth of yours to good use, and not for conversation, darling. So yes, I want you to go back to your apartment and sleep on it."

His crude honesty makes my heart race. "I understand, but I won't change my mind. I've made my final decision," I say, tucking a piece of hair behind my ear.

"Another trait we have in common … but one last thing before you go."

"Aha?"

"What do you expect from all of this, Blaire?"

"I don't expect anything because if I did, I would be sorely disappointed. Reality is never as good as one's imagination." I want to add that, as a young girl, I learned not to expect anything because each time I got my hopes up it would only bring utter disappointment and heartache. But I don't. Silence is golden after all.

He stares at me as if trying to figure out a difficult math equation. "You puzzle me, Blaire. Who are you? What are you?"

I look him in the eye and smile. "Complicated."

In the silence filled car as Tony drives me back to my apartment, I get the impression that he knows not to ask questions or chat with me. He probably understands better than I do that I need quiet at this moment.

Staring out the window, I follow the bright moon as we speed across the Long Island Expressway back to Manhattan. I watch her hide behind dark clouds, only to resurface minutes later and illuminate the night sky once more. Mentally and physically exhausted after an evening spent with Lawrence, I close my eyes and think of him. I think about the chill I felt as I left his house, the same prickling sensation behind my neck of being watched returning as I approached the car with Tony standing by the open door. And how, when I looked back toward the entrance, I found him watching me leave from the library window.

And that's when it hits me.

We never kissed.

chapter twenty-two.

The next afternoon …

EARLIER IN THE DAY, I CALLED Elly and asked her to meet me for lunch at our favorite sushi place. I want to tell her what is going on, and that I'm not going back to work. Well, at least not for the time that I'm supposed to be Lawrence's sidepiece.

I suspect it also has to do with the fact that I want to get out of my apartment. His green eyes, his voice, and the memories from yesterday keep tormenting me like a nightmare over and over again. I can't get them out of my head. I haven't called him, and I'm not exactly sure why. I guess part of me likes to play games, and I want to make him and his millions wait, or maybe I'm afraid that I imagined the whole thing.

Once we get to the restaurant, a cozy place in the Lower East Side that serves the best bento lunch box in the city, a hostess with long black hair guides us to a table at the back. A small block of wood that functions as a table is painted an opaque black and very low to the ground. We sit on long, cherry-red cushions that cover the floor, facing each other. House music is playing in the background, reminding me of my Buddha Bar's CDs back at home.

"So, how is your guitar player?" I ask Elly as I remove the paper wrapping from the chopsticks, split them in half, and rub them together to remove the splinters.

"I'd like to first say that I can't be held responsible for my behavior when under the influence of good music."

"*That* good, huh?" I ask.

She blushes. "Oh my God, Blaire … he's perfect. I couldn't wait the three-date minimum. I just couldn't."

I grin and place the chopsticks next to my plate. "You, my friend, suffer from rock star goggles."

She giggles. "Maybe. But seriously, I didn't plan on sleeping with him so soon. Things just happened."

"Oh, I bet they did. But how soon are we talking about here?"

She covers her burning cheeks with her hands and shakes her head, smiling. "Second date. And I mean it, Blaire! Things just happened. He had a small gig in a bar around NYU. After the show was over, a couple of his friends and their girlfriends went back to his apartment to hang out. At first we just made out for hours in his bedroom, you know? And, well, one thing led to the other … until—"

"Until he ended up plucking your G string?" I joke. We laugh out loud as she blushes some more.

She shakes her head and purses her lips, trying not to smile. "Like I'm going to tell you. I'm a lady, remember? I don't kiss and tell."

"Just be careful and don't forget to use protection, Elly. You don't want to catch something like chlamydia, or, God forbid, commitment."

She giggles. "Duh! Anyway, enough about me. Tell me what's new with you? How are things going with Ronan?"

My heart contracts painfully. "He's gone."

She frowns. "What do you mean he's gone? You were talking about him like three days ago."

I pause as our waiter places a bowl filled with steaming edamame in front of us. After we thank her and watch her leave, I resume our conversation.

"Yeah, well, it's over. He got too close for comfort," I say, surprised at how indifferent I sound.

"Oh-kay ... and? What's going on, Blaire?"

Surrounded by bamboo walls and the aroma of teriyaki sauce drifting in the air, I look Elly in the eye and reveal how shameless I truly am. "I don't know if you remember the guy at the restaurant? The one who asked to speak with me privately. Anyway, it doesn't matter. I met up with him yesterday and ... he offered me a shitload of money to sleep with him on a regular basis as long as I don't expect a marriage proposal from him when everything is said and done. So I said yes."

Elly almost spits out the hot tea in her mouth. "What did you just say?"

I lift the teacup to my lips and take a small sip of the smooth brew, feeling it burn my throat as it goes down. "Yep, I'm getting paid for as long as we're together. And get this—his assistant made me fax her a copy of my most up to date blood work and she sent me his, which was totally weird but at least I know he's clean and saf—"

She shakes her head, waving her hands to stop me from continuing. "Wait ... wait ... wait ... *WHAT?* You couldn't possibly have done something like that, Blaire."

I laugh. *My best friend is really naïve when it comes to me sometimes.*

"Believe it." I pause to put my cup down in front of me and make sure it's perfectly centered. "I went to his house yesterday, though I shouldn't call it a house because it's like the biggest place I've ever seen. Anyway, we had dinner, and he made his offer while he fingered me on the dining room table. I accepted. Apparently we understand each other very well."

"Please tell me this is a big joke," she says, disapproval voiced in every word of hers.

"Nope, it's as real as it gets."

She shakes her head a couple times, her chestnut curls bouncing. "I can't believe you're doing this."

"Well, you better come to terms with it, Elly, because I am."

"But what about Ronan? Because, trust me, you wouldn't have told me about him if you weren't serious. I know you, Blaire, even if you keep telling yourself that I don't."

"You're grasping at straws here. Nothing is going to make me change my mind, particularly a broke guy who I dated for a month. Besides, with Lawrence I get to continue living the lifestyle that I'm accustomed to. The lifestyle that I like. And now I get to quit working and just have fun."

"You're being serious, aren't you?"

"Yes, I'm being very serious. He's waiting for another call from me to tell him that I'm definitely doing it, and then it'll be a done deal."

After two years of being best friends, Elly knows that I have a tendency to shut people out, particularly after they say something I don't like. Yet, she knows that she's the only person who can get through to me, and her next words prove that she doesn't mind telling me like it is. "I could be wrong, Blaire, but I think there's a huge difference between what you usually do ... you know, date rich guys who you like ... and getting paid to fuck someone. I mean, do you even like the guy?"

"Doesn't matter. And in my opinion, it's pretty much the same. I've never loved any of those guys and I'm pretty sure none of them ever took me seriously. To them I was just a thing to look at and fuck. And like Walker said, they saw right through to the gold digger. So yes, in my opinion this is better because at least I don't have to pretend to love him so he'll take me shopping. Lawrence only wants my body and I only want his wallet. It's the perfect arrangement."

"Of course it matters! This will be just a guy paying money to fuck you like a ... like a—"

"Whore," I finish for her. And she's right. I *date*. I don't fuck around, and most importantly, I don't have time to fuck around, so no one-night stands for me. My body is my only tool, and spreading my legs open is my superpower. So if they want it, they better work for it—pay for it. Because, in the end, I want them to see me as an investment, and if I gave up the goods the moment they took me to a nice restaurant, why would they? The thrill would be gone.

Do I want to be the girl who gets to go on vacations in Rome? Or do I want to be the girl who gets her head pushed down while giving a blowjob to the asshole in the bathroom stall of a fancy club for a free drink?

Please ... why bother? Aim high and you'll reach the stars. Drink champagne and eat caviar.

Elly reaches for my hand and I let her take it. "I'm sorry, B ... I-I—"

I cover our linked hands with my free one, suddenly feeling cold. "It's okay ... don't apologize. I want this. And if you must know ... I *am* attracted to Lawrence. Very much so," I say, thinking back to yesterday and the way it felt being invaded by his punishing touch.

"But what about love, Blaire? Love is a beautiful thing."

"It's only beautiful when you're on the receiving end, Elly. It's hell when it's not reciprocated. Trust me, I know."

"Yeah, but that's part of the package. Love wouldn't be half as sweet if we didn't know pain, if we didn't know what it is to live without it. Listen, I know we're still super young to even think about it, but what about a family or kids someday? I mean we're not going to be twenty-three forever."

I shrug. "A girl I met during my first few days in the city used to always say it took the same kind of effort to fall in love with a rich man than with a poor man, so we might as well fall in love with the rich one."

"What a bitch."

"Maybe ... but at least she's a smart bitch."

And it's true. I've always known that *if and when* I get married, it'll be to money or someone who'll advance me in life. I've never really bothered with the fairytale dream of marrying my high school sweetheart or the love of my life. My parents apparently married for love and look how they ended up. Look how fucked up their lives turned out to be. *No, thank you.* I'd rather not be emotionally invested at all but enjoy all the perks of being in a relationship ... *kind of.*

Is Lawrence going to get me there? Probably not, but at least I won't have to deal with lunatics who think that they own me, or love me, because I make them orgasm. I'm not a fool. I know they don't love me one bit. They love the idea of me, and that's what I'm selling.

I won't be in danger of falling for him like I did with Ronan, but I'm cool with that. I don't want love ... I don't care if Lawrence loves me or not because I won't ever let myself fall in love. Love is dangerous. Love has the ability of breaking the unbreakable. Take Walker for an example. I didn't love him and he still managed to hurt me. And I, for one, won't ever be made vulnerable again. I won't. I can't.

As far as Lawrence goes, I've finally found someone who seeks the same kind of relationship I want.

chapter twenty-three.

IT'S BEEN TWO DAYS SINCE I last saw Lawrence. Two days since we made our agreement. When I told Elly that his assistant got in touch with me, I wasn't joking. She made me fax her my blood work, and she emailed me Lawrence's. She also went over the terms as to how I was going to be paid. Fifty percent would be deposited into my bank account at the beginning of a thirty-day cycle, and the other fifty at the end. That day, after I'd signed the contract and faxed it back to her along with my blood work, I went online to check if the money was there. Lawrence was a man of his word. Five hundred thousand dollars was sitting pretty alongside the rest of my savings.

I couldn't believe it.

I sat staring at my screen for a very long time, the numbers blending together, willing myself to move, but I couldn't. After a while, when it finally sunk in, I ran to the bathroom and threw up.

It wasn't the money that made me feel ill. It was what it represented.

I chose Lawrence over Ronan. If I were a normal girl, I would follow my heart and disregard what reason was telling me, but I'm not. Far from it actually. I fell for Ronan as much as I was able to ... as much as I could, but Lawrence ...

When I'm with him, I feel unburdened by expectations. I don't feel constricted. I don't feel like I have to be a better person to deserve him. I don't feel like my emotions are trying to get the better of me. Emotions aren't trying to choke the life out of me. No, with Lawrence it's all about pleasure, raw attraction, and desire—about the fine things in life. And those things aren't love, generosity, or selflessness.

With Lawrence, I'm allowed to be the real Blaire. I'm allowed to be the selfish girl who likes to put herself first, the girl who would rather have an expensive bag than a love letter.

The study in his Park Avenue townhouse is a lovely room: opulent, masculine, powerful—just like the man himself. I'm wearing a backless, little black dress. The front is tame, but the back is extremely revealing. I cross my legs, feeling my thighs rubbing invitingly. Power and wealth in this magnitude are a huge fucking turn on for me.

I sit in one of the plush wine-colored leather couches across from his desk as I recall the things we did the last time we saw each other. Each memory pushes Ronan out of my head, diminishing the guilt until I can pretend it's not there. Flushing, I remember the feel of his fingers moving inside me. After Lawrence pours two glasses of scotch, he makes his way back to this side of the room and hands me the drink before he takes a seat.

"Here," he says.

When I reach for it, our fingers graze and I feel the heat emanating from his body. The electricity. His black magic. Our eyes connecting, he watches me greedily as a faint smile plays on his lips.

I bite my lip. "Thank you."

He reclines lazily, an arm spread along the back of the couch while his free hand holds the tumbler with scotch, and studies me. "A penny for your thoughts," Lawrence says in that low and raspy voice of his. He looks relaxed, but I can tell he is anything but. He wants me. I can sense it in the way his muscles tense as he waits for my answer. I can see it in the way his wolfish eyes devour me, stripping me naked.

Before I answer, I take a moment to stare at the magnificent man in front of me, and the longer I do, the desire in his green gaze saturating my every thought, the easier it gets to ignore the Blaire who thought an afternoon spent with Ronan and his family was one of the best days of her life. The Blaire who thought life couldn't get any better than when she was in Ronan's arms and pure joy spread through her wildly. Yes, the more I stare at Lawrence, the easier it gets. And the selfish part of me wants to use Lawrence. I want to fuck Lawrence so hard, allowing him to come inside of me until it's his name and his taste branded on my lips, and not the memory of Ronan's tender touch.

I see no point in beating around the bush. "Where's your bedroom, or are we going to fuck here?"

"Blaire, Blaire, Blaire ... it doesn't have to be that way, you understand?"

"Then tell me how it's supposed to be because I'm afraid I don't understand. I'm trying to stick to your rules. To do what you expect and want from me."

"I remember my rules perfectly, but we can still enjoy each other's company while fucking. It's just you and me. A man and a woman seeking pleasure in the other. No games, no pretending. Can you do that?"

"No games and no pretending, huh? I thought you wanted my body, not my soul."

"I want Blaire."

"You might not like what's underneath it all, Lawrence," I warn him.

"Why don't you let me be the judge of that?" he says, removing his tie. I follow the movement of his hand as he tugs the silk and loosens the knot. When I lift my eyes, I find him watching me, waiting for my answer.

It's funny how life works.

People can come into your life—be a part of your life—yet never know the real you; have no fucking clue who you really are. Then one unexpected day you meet that person who, in one glance, has you figured out. There's no tainted judgment in his eyes, only acceptance. *And maybe understanding.* The need to be better, or pretend to be better is not there because you know he likes you for who you are—every ugly and broken part of you. That's how Lawrence makes me feel. And unlike Ronan, who made me want to be a better person for that month we spent together so I could deserve him, I know I don't have to put on a show with Lawrence.

I place the tumbler on the wooden coffee table in front of me. "Do you pray, Lawrence?"

He takes a sip before answering me, unfazed by the drastic change of subject. "I don't. You?"

"I used to until I realized God is deaf. Now every time I kneel, it isn't to pray."

His quiet laughter fills the room. "If the devil were a woman and had a name, I believe it would be Blaire."

I give him a cheeky smile. "You see, when I was a little girl I would plead to Him each night to make my parents stop fighting. To give my dad the strength he needed to stop drinking. To make my mom come back to me, or to take me away with her."

I get on all fours and crawl toward him unhurriedly, each movement deliberate. The Persian rug under my hands and knees is silky soft, tickling the sensitive skin of my palms. When I'm between his legs, I rise to my knees and run a perfectly manicured hand over his cock, digging my nails lightly as the bulge in his pants turns solid beneath my touch.

"Already so hard," I whisper before I put my head on his chest, and continue to rub him. In this position, I can hear his heartbeat get faster and louder with every decadent stroke of mine. I can feel him throbbing under my palm.

"I would beg him to make my parents notice me ... love me. But he never listened because nothing changed. One day I woke up and she was gone. That little girl who cried herself to sleep while holding her dearest stuffed animal died. The urge to cry disappeared. Whether my parents were home, or bothered to look at me, stopped hurting me. I couldn't give a fuck anymore. I grew up. I shed all my childish fantasies and finally understood how the real world worked. I learned that I could use my looks to get ahead. That values didn't matter when passion and greed were involved. That money spoke louder than words, and that emotions were pointless."

I raise my head and look him in the eye. "I've done very shameful things to get by, to get me where I am. Today that's kneeling in front of you, one of the richest men in the world, with your hard cock in my hand. Tomorrow might be someone richer than you, more powerful even, but that's who I am. I'm a survivor with my own set of rules. And not even your kindness will make me break them. And *that*, Lawrence, is the real Blaire," I say, my chest rising with each breath.

"What was its name?"

"Whose name?" I ask, confused.

"Of the stuffed animal?"

"Why do you care?" I stall, not wanting to share that part of me.

"Answer me," he orders.

"Winkler." As soon as the words slip from my tongue, I feel more exposed to him than ever before. I feel naked. "Why did you want to know that?"

The world seems to stop spinning on its axis, suspending all movement as I await his answer. He leans down to whisper in my ear, his lips grazing my neck infuse my body with warmth, "I like the real Blaire … it's her I want." His voice is as rough as sand paper and his breath as soft as a butterfly's wing, making my stomach flutter.

Nodding, our eyes connect and remain locked as I wrap one hand behind his neck, bringing his face closer to mine, and let the other continue to slowly rub his erection. As the fabric of his dress pants grazes the skin of my palm, wetness gathers between my legs. *Yeah, I want him too. Badly.*

"Take me to your room, Lawrence."

His green eyes spark with light, with heat … with life. "Your parents were fools. I notice you. I see you. And right now that's enough."

chapter twenty-four

HIS GAZE UNWAVERING, HE RAISES a hand and lets the back of his fingers trace the curve of my cheeks, my jaw, and my lips. A pleased Lawrence nods, a seductive smile appearing on his manly face. Without saying a word, he helps me stand and guides us through the white hallways of his house to his bedroom. We walk past more abstract paintings, modern sculptures, and Chinese vases filled with white orchids on antique looking tables. The only sound filling our ears is the clicking of my heels.

My hands sweat.

My pulse skyrockets.

This is it.

But as we near Lawrence's room, what seems to be a faraway memory washes through me, and it's Ronan's voice that I hear loud and clear ...

"Why me, Ronan?"

"Because when I look at you, I see everything I want and everything I need."

My chest contracts, but I won't let thoughts of Ronan and our time together foil what's about to happen. I lock those thoughts away in a deep, dark place. I'm here to sleep with another man. I'll finally be able to put him in my past—where he belongs.

When we're standing inside Lawrence's bedroom, I notice that it's quite neat. There are no piles of clothes thrown over a corner or draped over the brown leather armchair by the window. A large and seemingly comfortable bed covered in steely gray sheets is situated in the middle of the room. As I glance around, taking in every single detail from the gilded mirror on the left to the dark gray walls covered in more paintings, I notice a book left open and lying dormant on the nightstand.

I step away from the door, letting my fingers graze the expensive furniture. The opaque espresso colored wood feels cool to my touch and the black curtains feel like dark heaven in between my fingers.

Curious to see what he's reading, I walk toward the nightstand. About to reach for the book I hear him recite a poem about spring and cherry trees that I also know by heart.

Pleasure settles deep within my chest as I turn in his direction and smile for the first time since we left his study. He's propped lazily against a tall dresser, watching me with eyes that shine so bright in the semi-dark room as he rubs his chest, almost as if it's his cock in his hand.

"*Twenty Love Poems and a Song of Despair.* Pablo Neruda. One of my favorite poets of all time."

He smiles, nodding in the direction of the book. "I didn't peg you for a poetry kind of girl."

I shrug, trying to appear careless. "Since I had no one growing up, books became my friends, my passion. And poetry … poetry makes me understand myself."

Running a hand through my hair, I watch as Lawrence closes the space between us in two strides. He leans down and cups my face in his hands. His touch is sure and commanding, and I love it. "I'm done talking, Blaire. Get on your knees."

When our gazes collide, a mutual gravity pulls us together and the result is explosive—light obliterating. A battle of power and wills with no winner in sight because it seems that we both like playing this game too fucking much. I get down on my knees in front of him, looking up as I watch him unfasten his black leather belt, loosen the button of his pants and unzip them slowly. He frees his already hard cock and gives it a couple pumps, giving me the opportunity to take in the sheer size and beauty of his magnificent erection.

My mouth waters.

Blood rushes to my brain, muddling my senses.

My cheeks feel hot. My pussy pulsates with life, with want.

"Open wide." He grips my chin, raising it slightly and caressing my lower lip. "I'm going to fuck your mouth now."

His words might be an order, but it's me who has the control at this moment. It's me who chooses to reach for his cock and wrap both of my hands around it as I caress his length. I lean in, put him inside my mouth and give him a long suck, my tongue tracing the pulsating veins. When my lips are wrapped around the hot silky skin of his dick, Lawrence closes his eyes, looking like he's dying a delicious death. I pull him out and lick the head, tasting the salty flavor of his pre-cum as I hear a deep groan being torn from his chest.

The animalistic sound drives me insane. It's the fuel that lights my insides with shameless desire. Need and want fill my every pore. My knees burning, I bring a hand inside my thong and rub myself, spreading the moisture of my body along my swollen clit. Lightheaded with pleasure, I push him deeper until my lips touch his balls.

He takes his suit coat off and throws it on the floor. His tie and shirt next, his eyes watch me fuck myself with my fingers while I suck him like my favorite lollipop.

"Goddamn, Blaire."

He wraps his hands in my hair and thrusts harder and harder. Lifting his hips, he drives his cock farther into my mouth, fucking my mouth, owning my mouth, and I take him. I take him until I choke and pull him out, breathing heavily. After I wipe my chin off, I taunt him as I let the tip of my tongue trace the contour of his cock. "Is that all you've got, Lawrence? Stop being such a fucking gentleman and fuck my mouth. Make me want to fuck you like an animal. Use me."

"Fuck," he growls. "That's enough."

Lawrence helps me up, and I watch the way his cock shines, wet from my mouth. Knowing what he tastes like, sweet musk and salty sweat, makes me want him even more.

I need to feel him inside of me, so I reach out for him with my arms. "Stop staring at me, and fuck me."

He stops me with his hand. "No. Take this off first," he says gruffly as his finger caresses the material covering my shoulders. "Let me see you."

As soon as his request infiltrates my ears, the small hairs on my arms stand up. Staring at him, an inferno in his eyes they burn so brightly, I push the dress off my shoulders. I feel the dress slip from my arms and torso down to the floor, leaving me completely exposed to Lawrence's appraisal. In nothing more than a simple yet elegant black lacy thong, I stand there watching him watch me as he grabs his length and begins to stroke himself, admiring my body.

He's not the only one.

As he fucks his own hand, I absorb his unforgiving beauty. If I thought he was perfection wearing a suit, a naked Lawrence is magnificent. Wide and strong shoulders meant to carry the world. Perfectly toned muscles to pick you up and fuck you against the wall. Skin the color of honey. And his beautiful cock.

Lawrence is all man and nothing in between.

He circles me as though he is admiring a work of art. "Bend over the bed and spread your legs wide, Blaire," he orders.

I follow his instructions.

I walk toward the bed, place my hands on the expensive duvet that feels cold to the touch, and bend over. I stare ahead at the window filled with the lights from the city and wait for his next move.

A mixture of lust and anticipation makes lava run through me, and I feel as though I'm burning from the inside out. I'm about to turn around when I feel his naked torso behind me, his lips moving behind my ear. "Don't move."

I don't listen to him and turn my head just in time to see him grab the thin scrap of lace between my ass, pulling it to the side, and trace the head of his cock along my slit. We both watch it get soaked in my body's reaction to him.

"Feel how much I want you," he says roughly, rubbing his erection between my ass cheeks.

I groan, fisting the duvet tightly.

Lawrence lets go of his cock and surprises me by pulling down my thong until it's lying on the floor. After he discards it, he gets on his knees behind me and runs his hands along my legs. His touch is scalding. His touch is divine. His touch makes me shake, a devastating earthquake passing through me.

"Lawrence, please ..."

He pushes me forward until the front of my thighs touch the bed. I feel his hands palm my ass, spreading me open to his inspection, and then it's his tongue licking my clit and moving inside me ... sucking ... lapping ... fucking my pussy. He eats me from behind, like he can't get enough of me, and it's driving me wild.

He pulls me closer to him, burying his face in my ass and continuing to torture me with his tongue. Out of the corner of my eye, I can see him pumping his cock with his free hand—the furious flick of his wrist hypnotizing.

Fast …

Faster …

Harder …

Bringing us both closer to release. With my hands still on the bed, I watch as he releases me, stands up, and licks his lips that gleam with my desire before he wipes his mouth with the back of his hand.

"Turn around and lie down on your back," he orders, his chest heaving.

Breathing heavily, I don't miss the way his eyes flare with hunger when they land on my breasts, and lie down. He moves on top of me, covering my body with his, and kisses me. Our lips and tongues twirl aggressively, the flavor of my body on his tongue, but then it's all him. His taste. His essence.

He breaks the kiss.

Cupping my breasts in his hands, pinching my nipples, making them hurt as he showers my neck with sullied kisses, he growls, "I'm going to fuck you now, Blaire. And I'm going to fuck you so hard and so good that you'll forget all about our deal. It's not my money that you'll want, but my cock moving inside you, filling you. It's me you'll want."

I stare at his face so close to mine, grab his cock in my hand and guide him to my hot entrance. Desire makes my hands slightly tremble. "I want you, Lawrence," I say as I rub his head along my opening, wetting his dick. "So much."

"Not as much as I want you." He lowers his head and begins to suck my nipples in his mouth, licking and biting until they are deliciously tender. But I know he's not as in control as he would like me to think. Beads of sweat trail down his forehead and his jaw is tightly clenched as I continue to stroke him against my opening. I know how close he is to losing said control.

I let go of him to wrap a hand around his neck, pushing him down, closer to my mouth, and whisper in his ear. "Fuck me, Lawrence. I want to feel you inside me."

"I hope you're not delicate, darling, because I'm going to fuck you until I break you."

And then he loses what little restraint he has.

He stands up, grabs me by the ass with one hand and pulls me to the edge of the bed. He rubs his cock on my clit, watching it get wet before he slides all the way inside in one deep and hard thrust that pushes me backward. I curse, my eyes rolling back as he fills me completely.

Straightening my legs, he grips them by the ankles and spreads them open as wide as he can ... *and begins to fuck my brains out.* The grey sheets on the bed forgotten, the world outside these doors forgotten. We are lost in each other.

I raise myself on my elbows and watch as his glistening cock pumps in and out of me fast, faster, harder ... the head barely out before he drives back in, shoving me further into the bed with the aggressive and powerful thrusts of his hips. Skin against skin, I can feel him everywhere. Inside. Outside. My body, my soul—every membrane is taken over by this basic need to take, and take, and continue taking until I can't anymore.

I whimper.

I moan.

My body hurts, but it hurts so damn good.

I lift my gaze to stare at him as he keeps pounding into me, and watch as he lets go of one of my legs, placing it on his hard chest, slippery with sweat. He licks two of his fingers and brings them inside me. I groan. It's much too tight. He moves them along with his cock, stretching me until pain becomes unbearable pleasure. Until he utterly owns me.

"Good God, Blaire … the feel of you …"

I moan, my head twisting with the carnality of it, his fingers and his erection moving inside me. It aches. It's beautiful. It's decadent. We live through our bodies with every caress, every bead of sweat, every glance, and every touch until we can't go on any longer.

"Lawrence … don't stop … don't stop … I'm … I'm—"

I can't finish my sentence because his mouth suddenly covers mine, kissing me as hard as he's fucking me, and I come undone. Like two planets violently colliding with one another, the power of my climax wipes out every thought, word, and action from my mind except the pleasure being torn from within me.

Cursing, Lawrence lets go of my legs and grabs my ass painfully, pulling me toward him and fucking me with wild and total abandon. I wrap my legs around his waist and hold onto his shoulders as he pistons in and out of me without mercy. My nails dig into his skin as I bite his shoulder forcefully. Our bodies are covered in sweat; the room coated in the smell of sex.

I moan.

He curses.

When he's about to come, he pulls out just in time to spill his seed on my stomach as a mighty groan rips from his chest. Closing his eyes, he tips his head back and gives himself a few final pumps, emptying himself on me. After a few slow seconds pass by, our fast breathing decreases and he opens his eyes, staring at me.

And what I see takes me by surprise.

His eyes laced with concern, he covers my body with his as his elbows encase my head. Pushing some of my hair that is stuck with sweat off my face, he asks, "Did I hurt you?"

I smile and shake my head. "No … but," I lower a hand and wipe some of his cum off my stomach. Bringing it to my lips, I lick it clean before adding, "But you did make me forget all about that bank account of yours."

He groans as he sees me lick his cum off my lips. "Fucking deadly … that's what you are."

Then his lips cover mine once more.

chapter twenty-five.

NAKED, I'M LYING ON MY STOMACH, feeling drowsy after a sleepless night of fucking. The soft pillow under my cheek invites me to fall asleep, when I feel Lawrence place a soft kiss between my shoulder blades. My sore lips form a lazy smile as I remember all the wicked things his mouth did to me last night.

"Morning," he says close to my ear. The clean smell of his expensive aftershave fills my nostrils. It replaces the one of sweat and sex that permeates the air in the room and lingers on my skin and pillow.

I turn over and open my eyes, staring at him. He's already showered and dressed for work. His eyes on me, I take a moment to admire how handsome he looks. He's wearing a navy-blue suit with a simple but elegant white dress shirt and the cutest of ties I've ever seen. I reach for the tie, grab it, and let my fingers caress the soft silk. "Penguins, Lawrence?"

He chuckles. "Traditional, darling."

"Only you could wear a Hermès tie and still manage to look so dashing." Letting go of the tie so I can wrap my fingers in his soft hair, I bring his mouth closer to mine. "Kiss me."

"More? Aren't you sated after last night and this morning?" He smiles.

I shake my head, our mouths not even an inch apart. "No …
I want you again." I lean forward, biting his lower lip.

"You eager little thing." I feel his hand move between my
legs. I enjoy the way his pupils expand with something dark,
something fascinating as he watches me open them to welcome
his touch.

"Always so ready for me." His fingers enter me slowly one,
two, three times before he pulls out and traces my neckline with
them, covered in my wetness. "I wish I could. But I can't right
now, Blaire. I have an important meeting in less than an hour
that I can't miss."

"Fine, be that way," I pout. I let go of his fingers, stretch on
the bed, and place one arm under my head. Slowly, I let my free
hand roam the valley between my breasts down to my pussy,
shamelessly exposing myself to him … provoking him …
taunting him. "I thought you might want to get your money's
worth."

Lawrence ignores my crass comment as his eyes land on my
chest. He leans forward and kisses the side of my left breast. "I
hurt you."

I look down and notice a bite mark where he kissed me a
second ago, the red bruise beginning to turn a splotchy purple. I
lick my lips and stare at him. "I liked it … I liked everything
about last night, and I thought you did too."

"Last night was utter perfection, Blaire." He caresses my
cheek softly. "But I have to be more careful with you."

"Why? You don't have to. I loved every single thing you did
to me, Lawrence."

I remember how it felt the second time we had sex. He took
me viciously from behind. He was as unforgiving as I was
unrepentant. He took. I gave. He bit. I drew his blood.

"There's something about you that makes me lose my mind. Something that makes me lose control. And I don't like it."

"Well, I liked it very much."

He shakes his head, his eyes landing on the clock sitting by the metallic lamp. "I have to go, it's getting late but before I forget, call Gina if you need anything. She's been instructed to follow your orders."

I roll and get off the bed, making my way toward my clothes that are still lying on the floor. My bare feet sink in the plush carpet as I cross the room and grab my bra. I put it on as I turn in his direction.

"I must say, Lawrence, you're making it really hard for me to feel like I'm being sexually exploited here."

He raises an eyebrow, a faint smile spreading across his face. "Am I now, Blaire?"

"Yep. You fuck as good as you look."

He chuckles. "Your honesty, Blaire. It's a breath of fresh air, even if sometimes it can be—"

"Too much?" I interrupt him, thinking about all the ways he played with my body. I don't feel anything for him—that's a given. However, after last night I can easily say that I love fucking him. His hands. His kisses. His cock. Destruction. Obscurity. Lawrence, my decadent oblivion, made me feel nothing but pure selfish ecstasy. *He also made me forget* ...

"Maybe I need a good spanking? But you can't take it too far ... we don't want you to pull a muscle or anything," I tease, knowing perfectly well that Lawrence is in his prime both physically and sexually.

He comes to stand in front of me. "I must say that your concern for my welfare touches me deeply." His smiling eyes are bright with humor as sarcasm rolls off his tongue. "That's a first for me."

I close the space between us until my breasts graze the front of his chest and our lips aren't even an inch apart, placing my hand on the front of his pants. "Poor Lawrence," I coo against his skin. "I better be gentle with you."

"How about I tell you how much I want to take care of you? How much I care about your," I pause and move slightly back to stare at him as I caress the outline of his cock ever so gently, "*welfare.*"

Without saying a word, he lowers his hand and wraps his fingers around my wrist. We stand still, time dragging its feet like morning lovers, his touch etching on my skin. For a moment, I believe he's going to remove my hand brusquely, but to my surprise he raises it to his smiling mouth and places a soft kiss in my palm. "What am I going to do with you, little rogue?"

I smirk. "Spoil me, of course."

"Which reminds me …"

I watch as he pulls out a long red case with gold details framing the edges of the box from the inside pocket of his suit. *Cartier.* The thought of what's inside of it makes my blood pump faster. I smile as my eyes widen. I look up and find his green gaze on me. He's watching me carefully —studying me— analyzing me. For a second, I'm embarrassed by how obvious I'm being, but then I remember why I'm here and the mortification I felt a moment ago disappears. A virginal blush spreads across my cheeks while I hope that he can see the greediness in my eyes just in case he had any doubts about my feelings for him. This is the whole reason why I am with him, after all.

He opens the gift and retrieves the sparkling necklace lying on a bed of white satin, carelessly discarding the box on the floor. Staring at me, he asks, "May I?"

I nod and bite my lip as I take in the diamonds set in the thin two-tiered white gold chain. It's a lovely piece of jewelry and, like so many before, it reminds me of myself. This cold, lifeless object shines. It's expensive and seemingly perfect, but is it?

As soon as he places the necklace around my neck, an urge to remove it, almost as if my skin were developing an allergic reaction to the metal, comes over me. The gold chains feel as though they are shackles, binding me to Lawrence, and I don't like it one bit. I'm about to thank him and take it off, but the way he's looking at me makes me hesitate.

"What is it? Don't you like it?" he asks, his brows furrowing.

The memory of a Hello Kitty watch and how it meant more to me than any necklace ever will crosses my mind, but as quick as the thought comes, I dismiss it. That memory belongs in the past, and that's where it will stay.

I force a smile as I place a hand on my neck. "It's perfect. I would say that you didn't have to get me something so expensive, but that would be a lie, so thank you."

I stand on my tiptoes and lean over, kissing him on the cheek. His hands instantly land on my naked hips, gripping them tightly. "If I'm going to get one of those every time I give you something, you leave me no other choice but to spoil you, after all."

"Careful … you might go broke," I tease him.

"One more thing."

Lawrence lets go of me before he walks to the nightstand. Puzzled, I watch him retrieve a piece of paper resting on the smooth wood surface then make his way back to me.

He hands me an envelope. "Here."

I raise an eyebrow as I take the envelope and open it. My eyes immediately land on a black credit card with my name on it. There's one thing that every self-proclaimed gold digger knows and that is that the small black plastic card in my hands is the Bible of credit cards. It has no limit and only the very wealthy have access to it. I mean, you could pretty much charge a Ferrari on it and no one would bat an eyelash.

I look up, our eyes meeting.

"Have I finally managed to leave you speechless?" he asks, laughter in his voice.

"You bet."

"Go to Bergdorf's and buy yourself a whole new wardrobe. Shoes, bags … whatever you want. I don't want to see you wearing clothes that other men have paid for, or have had the pleasure of seeing you wearing it before me. Understood?"

"Are you sure? That's going to be a lot of money, Lawrence. I have very expensive taste, you know."

He leans down and kisses me on the mouth. The kiss is quick but still manages to take my breath away in its intensity. "I'm sure. Don't worry about the price or how much it is. I can afford it, Blaire."

I raise my hand in salute, teasing him. "Aye aye, Captain."

He surprises me by spanking me on the ass, a playful glimmer in his eye. "Another thing." He fiddles with the waistband of my thong.

"Yes?"

"When you're in my bed, I want you naked. You, me, and nothing else, so don't bother wearing these silly things in the future. There's no point. Got it?"

Have you ever watched the flame of a candle burn? The flicker twirling fluidly as it dances in the air without restraint, its beauty hypnotizing. You can't look away. You don't want to. That's how I feel at this moment as Lawrence and I stare at each other. His eyes draw me in, searing through me and leaving a trail of heat behind.

My mouth dry, I nod. "Am I going to see you tonight?"

As soon as the words leave my mouth, I realize that I *want* to see him again.

Lawrence shakes his head. "Not tonight. I have a … business dinner of sorts that I can't miss. I'll see you tomorrow evening."

I shrug my shoulder, pretending that his refusal doesn't sting, that I didn't sense a lie underneath his excuse. "Okay … can I ask you a question before you leave?"

"Yes."

"Are we exclusive or can we see other people when we're not together? Not that I plan to, of course, but I'd like to know where things stand," I say, thinking of Walker and how he blindsided me.

"Blaire, we're fucking, and hopefully having a great time together. Whatever you choose to do on your free time doesn't concern me, and vice versa."

After we kiss goodbye, I make my way to the bathroom. I should take a shower, but without Lawrence here I feel like the intruder that I am and just want to go home. I'm brushing my teeth with the new toothbrush Lawrence's cleaning lady left for me when my eyes land on the necklace. It reminds me of the conversation we had after having sex for the first time …

We're naked and lounging drowsily on his bed, sharing a glass of red wine when he asks me, "Have you always slept with men for money?"

"Yes and no. I'm usually in relationships with them. Some last longer than others. Walker, the guy you saw me with at the Met the night I met you, was probably my longest one."

"Do you need the money? Debts? Is that why you do it?"

"Not really. I just like it." I smile as I let my palms caress the cool softness of the silk covering the mattress.

"I see. No noble cause for fucking men like me, and selling your body," he says wryly.

"Nope. I let you fuck me because I like how much you pay me."

Lawrence places the wine glass on the table before he turns to kiss my chin. He slaps my ass playfully, then sits up with his back reclined against the headboard.

"Then let's get my money's worth."

I stretch myself as though I were a cat and watch him out of the corner of my eye as he begins to stroke his cock with his hand. Getting on my knees, I straddle him as both of us watch his erection enter me slowly ... the way the head opens me to his invasion ... the penetration made easy by the mixture of new and old arousal from my body. I lean forward and hold onto the headboard as he fills me completely and say breathlessly, "Yeah, let's."

Once I rinse my mouth, I look at myself in the mirror. All I see is an ambitious girl with almond-shaped blue eyes and midnight hair who is willing to give up just about anything to achieve her goals.

I wonder how far is she willing to go to achieve them.

But what are those? Happiness? Wealth?

As I continue to stare at my reflection, I wonder if I even know what I'm chasing after anymore. I look so lost. The bitch inside me tells me that I may look lost but satisfied, and to check out the place. It's huge, even for a townhouse. She also tells me that Ronan would never be able to give me any of this, so to stop playing the smallest maudlin violin in the world and get on with it. I feel like crying, but the tears won't fall, and that's all right. Because even if it were possible for me to do so, my tears shouldn't be allowed. Tears are for people who are sorry for their actions.

And I'm not.

Life is a show where my soul is naked, but I'm covered in lies.

And I'm okay with that because, in life, only the fittest survive.

chapter **twenty-six.**

LAWRENCE OFFERED ME THE SERVICE of one of his chauffeurs to drive me home, but I declined politely. I want some time alone to clear my head after everything that has happened in the past twenty-four hours, and the last thing I need is someone to look at me with judgment pouring out of their eyes because they know I've just spent the night having sex with their boss. Not that I think Tony would judge me, or that I would normally care, but I'm just not feeling up for it.

Riding the elevator to my floor, I can't wait to get to my apartment so I can get out of my clothes and take a long hot shower. Maybe relax by reading a book, or take a much-needed nap. But the moment I step out of the elevator, I know that isn't possible.

Ronan is sitting with his back against my door, waiting for me. As our eyes connect, I know it's time to face the music.

When I begin walking toward him, Ronan stands up from his place on the floor and turns to face me. My heart beats angrily against my chest, but I disregard my body's response to him; the way my fingers itch to tame the familiar wild golden brown hair that frames his boyishly handsome face. *Mind over matter, Blaire. Mind over matter.* Yet, as I close the space between us, I feel as though I can't breathe because of the pain gathering in the center of my chest.

"So that's it, huh? Not even an explanation as to why we're done. Just a fucking text?"

I cross my arms and lift my chin in challenge. "I thought it was best. I hate theatrics such as this."

"No, that isn't it, Blaire, and you know it. I got too close, made you feel something real for once, and so the first chance you got, you ran."

"Don't think so highly of yourself," I drawl. "We were fucking and having fun. That was all."

He shakes his head. "Bullshit. You're a fucking coward who's too afraid to let someone in. So instead of dealing with your feelings like an adult, you pushed me out."

Anger boils inside me because the truth behind his words hurts. The funny thing is, I *know* he has every right to be angry with me because of the way I behaved toward him, but I can't help myself. Never ruffle the feathers of a spiteful woman because she will not only want to hurt you, but she will want to draw your blood.

"Yikes, you're going for the jugular, aren't you? Poor Ronan … I must've really hurt you, but I did warn you. I told you I wasn't good for you."

"Yeah, I guess the fucking joke is on me for thinking that there was something real. Something I fucking needed … something I *wanted* so bad underneath your flawless exterior, but I was obviously mistaken. There's nothing there."

"You only saw what you wanted to see, Ronan. I never pretended to be something I'm not," I say, suddenly feeling like crying because I remember how he used to look at me how different it was from any other guy before.

"How can someone as beautiful as you are have no heart?"

196

I laugh bitterly. "I have no heart. I killed it. You and I were never meant to be together, so get it out of your fucking head. Besides, you'll be okay. You'll forget me in a couple of weeks."

"Be out of my mind? Forget you?" He runs his hands through his hair, tugging at the ends. "I've thought about you every single day since I've met you. Every part of me aches for you, cries for you, craves you."

I crack. "Stop it! Stop it! Stop it!"

In a moment of weakness, I wonder what would happen if I ended things with Lawrence and asked Ronan to forgive me and give me another chance. But I don't because it wouldn't change the outcome.

God, what a fool I am.

I can already see it unfolding. If I let him in completely, he would break down all my walls one sweet kiss at a time and I would fall madly and deeply in love with him and the promise of a future together. I would think that I've finally found what I've been searching for all my life. And then one day he would look into my eyes and nothing would happen. Nothing. His eyes wouldn't dance in the light when they landed upon my face. What he once thought beautiful would be ordinary. With my phony and expensive exterior infiltrated, he would realize how worthless, how ugly I am on the inside and he would leave me like everyone else has. Or maybe I would grow bored, like my mother did with her marriage to my father. Maybe I'd want that Chanel bag he couldn't afford but someone like Lawrence could. The end result would always be the same, proving how unworthy of love I truly am.

Ronan's eyes soften for the first time since I've arrived. "Don't do this, Blaire. Don't give up on us."

"You're blind, Ronan," I mutter, my voice shaking.

"No, you're the one who's blind, Blaire. Give me the chance to show you what I see. Give me a chance to prove to you that what we have is something special."

As we continue to stare at each other, anger fills me once again, corroding my heart and soul. His kind words, sharp as a serrated knife, manage to hurt me, cut me open. His truthful words are cruel, but such is the perverse nature of honesty. It's rarely painless and always full of baggage.

I take the last few steps that separate us as opposing thoughts spin in my head.

Once I'm standing in front of him, I notice that Ronan is watching me warily. Good. He should be worried. Adrenaline pumps through my veins. A cool draft from the air conditioner envelops the small space between us, but I feel feverish. What I do next can't be blamed on thoughtlessness or be classified as one of those spur-of-the moment-kind of things. Nope. It's calculated. It's meant to hurt him. It's meant to show Ronan that I have the upper hand and not him. It's meant to show him how ugly I am, shattering his noble and bogus opinion of me once and for all. He thinks I'm blind? No, it's him. And I'll show *him* just how blind *he* is.

I give him my best smile—the one that makes grown men lose their mind and forget their values as long as they get to put their cock inside of me. Pushing myself against him, his hands instantly cup my ass. The length of our bodies glued, I rub myself on his hardness and feel the way it swells for me, the way my body instantly ignites for him.

I place my hands on his shoulders and lean forward until our mouths are not even an inch apart. I can smell the woodsy smell of his cologne and feel the warmth of his breath against my lips. I can see the light dusting of golden freckles adorning the crest of his nose, and most importantly, I can sense our need for each other coating the air in the empty hallway.

"You say that I'm blind, Ronan, but I'm not. I know perfectly who I am. It's you who can't see it, won't believe it."

And that's when I kiss him. It's a hard kiss meant to punish him, to bring him to his knees, and it starts out like that. Our tongues clashing, fighting for power to render the other useless. But the moment Ronan lets go of my ass and cups my cheeks lovingly in his hands, I come undone. It's he who punishes me with his tenderness.

His passion.

His beauty.

His kisses full of light.

He's the one to break the kiss by pulling back slightly, desperation and need vibrating through his touch. "You feel that, Blaire? How can you deny that? This thing, this pull between us isn't a temporary thing. It isn't going anywhere, and you know it. You can tell lies to your head and maybe believe them, but you can't lie to your heart, to what's deep inside of you. It always knows the truth. Now, tell me to my face that you don't care about me. That you really want me out of your life. I'll be gone and I won't ever bother you again."

I shake my head wordlessly but he doesn't seem to care. "What are you so afraid of? Tell me."

I shake my head once more.

"Tell me, Blaire."

Forcefully, I push his hands away as I try to swallow the tight knot that has formed in the back of my throat. Lies sit on my tongue ready to be fired at him, but the honesty shining in his eyes forbids me to deceive him. "You, okay? You! I'm scared shitless of what you make me feel, what you make me want." My voice breaks.

"Don't be ... don't be afraid of me."

"Oh, Ronan. When will you learn?"

"Never."

I touch my burning lips, feeling the ghost of his mouth upon them as we stare at each other. His words resonate deep within me, destroying my resolve with each second that passes by, but then I catch myself wanting to believe them. Like the Pied Piper of Hamelin and his song, his seductive words want to take me away to a place of no return, and I won't let him. I won't.

"It doesn't matter. Do you want to know something about me, Ronan?" I ask, pushing myself closer to him again.

Ronan grips my hips painfully, his fingers leaving soft, red indentations there. I lean forward and kiss his neck before I whisper against his skin, "I fucked a man the entire night." I kiss his Adam's apple and feel it tremble under my lips. "And it wasn't for love." I kiss him behind his left ear, letting my tongue trace the soft skin there as I taste the saltiness of his sweat. "I can still feel him moving inside me ... I can still taste his flavor on my tongue... so you think I'm a good person, huh?" I grab one of his hands, bringing it between my legs, and guiding his fingers with mine to touch me and rub me there. The warmth of his touch seeps through the lace of my underwear. "What if I told you that you could have me as many times as that man did if you could afford me?"

Ronan pushes me away forcefully, our hands separating. "Enough, Blaire ... enough."

I ignore him and keep going. I want to open his eyes and shatter all his illusions so he can finally see me for who I am.

A monster.

"I'm a gold digger, you know? I fuck for money." I stare at him, rejoicing when I notice his taut jaw because it means I'm finally getting to him. "And frankly, it doesn't look like you could ever pay my price. So, Ronan, let me ask you again. How much do you like me? How special do you think I am? Do you still think I'm blind? Because in my book, it looks like you're the blind one."

There. I hope that shuts him up.

I feel completely dead on the inside. And if I wasn't before by my own doing, the way he's looking at me in this moment finishes the job. Like a coward, I'd like to lower my gaze and not be an unwilling witness to his judgment, but I don't think I can. There's something magnificent, awe-inspiring, when you watch a man lose his way in anger … in hate. You can't help but wish to be part of the wreckage left behind by his ire.

Silence fills the space between us, stretching like a never-ending ocean. We're standing in front of each other, our bodies close enough to touch, yet we've never been farther apart.

"I take that back. I take everything back that I said earlier." He eyes me up and down, disgust carried in each syllable he utters. "You're not worth it."

My breath is shaky. My palms are sweaty. A tempest of tension, desire, fury, and pain roars inside me.

"I'm glad you finally realize it," I say as I unlock my apartment, walk inside and close the door behind me, shutting Ronan out of my life once and for all.

After I strip naked, I stand in front of my mirror and take in my appearance. With the back of my hand, I remove the remaining ruby red lipstick from my bruised lips, smudging it across the left side of my face. My eyes sparkle with tears that won't fall. Ronan's words spin inside my head like a revolving door, paralyzing me. But at least he knows now what kind of person I am. He finally sees me the way I see myself.

I continue to stare at my reflection as I ignore the soreness between my legs. I wasn't born a monster, though my choices certainly have made me one. But I can't stop myself. I can't. Causing pain to others when I'm suffering soothes me.

I wish I could cry, but nothing happens. I hate myself. I tell myself I'm worth it, but I don't believe it. The vicious cycle continues.

Over …

And over …

And over …

chapter twenty-seven.

Lawrence

AS I WAIT FOR MY DATE TO join me for dinner, I think of Blaire and chuckle. She's a walking contradiction without a doubt, but maybe that's part of her charm. A femme fatale with the eyes of an old soul and a playful smile that is sure to rob a man's heart. This morning before I got out of bed, I spent a couple of minutes watching her sleep. I wanted to touch her again. I wanted to pull her close to me and smell her feminine perfume, maybe wake her up and fuck one more time, but somehow I knew that I shouldn't. She isn't mine. So I contented myself with staring at her like a lovesick puppy while she slept in my bed. Without an ounce of makeup on her face and her black hair spread across the pillow in wild abandon, she appeared so young and carefree. Innocent almost. But then my eyes drifted to her naturally red tinted lips. No innocent girl could suck a man off the way she did.

Her memory alone makes my cock stir.

But it's not her body I crave; it's her. I crave the way she makes me feel. She makes me forget. She has brought back laughter into my life after so many years without it, and like a starved man, I want more—I need more. And if I have to pay for each kiss, each touch, each smile of hers, so be it. I don't care. At least she's honest enough to admit that all she wants from me is my money.

I chuckle because a slip of a girl with soulful blue eyes is turning me into a pathetic son of a bitch. I'm about to reach for my glass of wine when I hear my date speak.

"Hi Laurie."

I place my napkin on the table, push the chair back and stand up.

"When will you stop calling me that?" I ask, our eyes meeting.

"Never, silly man."

She smiles as she leans forward and kisses my cheek. The moment her lips touch my skin, the same feelings that have haunted me and been my only companions for close to ten years return in full force.

Sometimes I think that I'm finally free of her.

But I know that my freedom is just an illusion.

chapter twenty-eight.

THERE'S SOMETHING TO BE SAID about being Lawrence's shiny fuck toy and getting paid to be one. Lawrence doesn't fuck or screw.

He fornicates ... like an animal.

It's dirty.

Wild. Unrepentant. Possessive.

It's pleasure and pain all at once.

And me? I've seen him twice since our first night together and I can't help but want him more after each time. I crave the way he numbs everything with his hard, gorgeous cock. I crave the way his hands worship me after they've punished me. And his tongue ...

God have mercy on my vagina.

My cheeks burn just thinking about him. I should be ashamed by how much I like being used by him, but I'm no hypocrite. I love it. And the fact that our feelings aren't involved makes it that much sweeter. Who doesn't like a fast, angry fuck without the obligatory niceties? And let's not forget about the expensive and frivolous gifts he leaves on the nightstand table waiting for me after a night spent on my back.

Or knees.

"I'm almost done!" I shout, hoping that Lawrence hears me. I was supposed to meet him in his Park Avenue townhouse an hour ago, but he got stuck in a meeting that ran longer than expected, making him late. Since he was already in Midtown for business, he decided to pick me up on his way home.

When he first walked in, I wanted to laugh out loud. It was quite difficult to watch such a masculine and rugged looking man being surrounded by all my frilly things. He looked like a fish out of water. I smile, shaking my head and dismissing the memory.

Where the hell are my shoes?

After I locate my crystal-encrusted pumps under an old Louie bag I haven't used in ages, I put them on. I grab a clutch that matches my shoes, and fill it with cash, I.D., lip-gloss and keys.

"I'm ready," I say, walking out of my bedroom. I hope he likes the simple, but very sexy little black dress I'm wearing. It clings to my curves seductively, showing off my legs and hourglass figure without being too slutty or screaming that I'm looking to get laid.

His head is down and I watch him as he types away on his—

"Oh my God. Is that a Blackberry? I had no idea people still used those ancient things," I say, incredulity ringing in my voice.

He stops typing and looks up at the same time. "Yes, Blaire. People still use the—"

He stops talking, an arrested expression on his face, the moment his eyes land on me. "Them." I walk toward him, pleased by how affected he seems. A small smile plays on my lips as I watch the way his eyes darken with desire. I watch him hungrily roam my face, breasts, hips, every single part of my body without any shame. The obvious admiration written in his every feature makes me feel wicked. Daring. Playful. Makes me feel like teasing the man who looks like an orgasm on legs.

By the time I make it to the couch, he's already standing. "What do you think? Do you like it?" I ask as I begin to twirl painfully slow. I want him to admire and crave every slope and curve of my body.

He surprises me when he forcefully grabs me by the waist and pulls me close to him until our chests are touching. Even in my six-inch heels he towers over me, and I have to tilt my head back to be able to look him in the eye. Lust instantly thickens the air around us, making it harder to breathe. I run a hand through my hair, feeling nervous for the first time tonight. Lawrence leans down, grabs my face roughly between his hands and says, "Insolent girl. I'll show you how much I like it when you're in my bed."

The images of him filling my body in every possible way swim in my head, my every thought drowning in desire. "Sounds like that could be dangerous, Lawrence," I tease.

He laughs, and the sound is rich and throaty and so very delicious. "The best things in life always are. But I get the feeling that you like dangerous."

I'm about to answer when he speaks once more.

"Do you really want to keep talking?"

I shake my head.

"Good because I've wanted to do this since I first walked in."

"What's that?" I murmur against his mouth, our breaths mingling together.

"This," he says before his lips land on mine.

His kiss is like dark chocolate, bitter and laced with sweetness—an aphrodisiac. It's darkness and light all at once. His kiss doesn't ask. It takes. It demands total surrender, and I give it to him. I give him everything, whatever he wants. And I'm lost to it all. I'm lost to his tongue, to his lips, to his teeth that bite and feel like they draw blood. It hurts. It's paradise. It makes my knees go weak. And it erases the memory of every kiss before him …

Except one.

When he pulls away, looking satisfied, I whisper breathlessly against his mouth, "You're right."

"Sweetheart, I'm always right. But what do you mean?"

"I *like* dangerous." I grab the back of his head and pull him in for another kiss.

When we step out of my building, cool air caresses our skin. I turn to look at Lawrence, only to find him watching me with those striking green eyes of his. "What are you thinking about?" I smile.

Without breaking eye contact, he leans down, kisses the tip of my shoulder, and whispers in my ear, "Fucking you."

My pulse picks up and my body buzzes with excitement as a hot blush covers my cheeks. I can still feel the smile on my lips when I spot the familiar black Rolls Royce parked outside my building. Expecting to see Tony, my gaze immediately goes to the man wearing an old-looking black suit I've seen before standing by the open passenger door, waiting for us.

When our eyes connect, shock hits me hard in the face, robbing me of the power to move. For a moment, I'm stunned. Speechless. I blink a couple of times to make sure that my eyes are not mistaken and that I'm not imagining things.

Fuck. Fuck. Fuck. Fuck. Fuckity fuck fuck.

Watching me with eyes that could potentially destroy me is the last man I hoped to ever see—the only man who ever made me want more.

Ronan.

To be continued ...

acknowledgements.

I WANT TO THANK MY HUSBAND and family for loving me and supporting me through it all. I love you more than words can ever describe.

Next I would like to thank each and every single person that helped me in creating Easy Virtue—my very special group of BETA readers. Without your help and feedback this book would have never been completed. Amy, Mint, Luna, Bridget, Ana Rita, Rosalinda, Melissa S., Megan, Chelsea, Katherine, Melissa E, Jennifer, Deana, Trisha—EV wouldn't be what it is without you! I love you, girls.

Luna, I want to thank you so much for helping me out with all the teasers. You're truly talented and such a giving, beautiful person. Thank you! <3

Jennifer, my beautiful and talented editor, thank you so much for being there for me and for dealing with my crazy. I wrote Easy Virtue, but it was your work and magic that made it readable and enjoyable. THANK YOU.

Ryn, I want to thank you for perfecting EV with your proofreading services. It was a pleasure working with you! I hope we can do it again.

Kassi, thank you so much for making EV pretty and for answering all my questions. You were always there for me when I had a question with regards to the formatting, and, as always, your work is exceptional and reliable.

Regina, the cover you created for EV took my breath away—It's perfect. Your unbelievable talent humbles me and I can't wait to see what you come up next with my next cover. Also, thank you so much for working tirelessly on this cover. I know it took us a while to get there, but it's perfection.

Kelley and Ashley, thank YOU!!!

BIG, BIG SHOUT OUT to my girls in the ARSEN Discussion and Spoiler group. You guys have made that place something really special. Here is to hoping EV gives us as many hours of discussion as Arsen did. MAD LOVE TO YOU ALL!

I want to give a special shout out to all the bloggers and individuals that helped spread the word. No one would know about my novel if it weren't for your help. I would be nothing without your help. Thank you for believing in me (again) and in EASY VIRTUE.

Also, special thanks to The Rock Stars of Romance for organizing a kick-ass cover reveal and blog tour. Lisa and Milasy, you lovely ladies are so wonderful to work with. Also, thank you to Natasha from Natasha is a Book Junkie for answering all my questions and for your help! Amy, Trish, Jennifer, and Jesey from Schmexy Girl Book Blog, thank you so much for your support! Big thank you to Angie from Angie's Dreamy Reads, Christine from Shh Mom's Reading, Sharon, Jenny and Gitte from Totally Booked, Yamara, Bethany from HEA Bookshelf, Dawn from Up all Night, Kathy from Love Words and Books, and Sophie from Bridger Bitches Book Blog.

To FYW, thank you for all your help! Liquidate that! ;)

Thank you to all my family and friends for putting up with me and for always being there for me. I know I'm forgetting someone and if I do know that I'm truly sorry. I love all the encouraging words, the lovely words from every single person that has stopped by my page and said hello. I love every single one of you.

This book would not be anything without the support and love from all of you. Thank *you* so, so much.

Made in the USA
San Bernardino, CA
27 July 2016